THE TROUBLE WITH SARAH GULLION

MICHAEL P. HARDING

D1642882

THE
BLACKSTAFF
PRESS
BELFAST AND ST PAUL, MINNESOTA

ACKNOWLEDGEMENTS

Grateful acknowledgement is made to Faber and Faber Limited for permission to quote from 'Whatever You Say Say Nothing' from *North* by Seamus Heaney. The author acknowledges the hospitality of the Tyrone Guthrie Centre at Annaghmakerrig while the story was being written, and is especially grateful to Brendan Harding for his encouragement and understanding.

First published in 1988 by
The Blackstaff Press Limited
3 Galway Park, Dundonald, Belfast BT16 0AN, Northern Ireland
and
Box 5026, 2115 Summit Avenue, St Paul, Minnesota 55105, USA
with the assistance of
The Arts Council of Northern Ireland

Printed by The Guernsey Press Company Limited

British Library Cataloguing in Publication Data
Harding, Michael P.
The trouble with Sarah Gullion.
1. Title
823'.914[F]

Library of Congress Cataloging-in-Publication Data
Harding, Michael P., 1953–
The trouble with Sarah Gullion.
1. Title.
PR6058.A6368T76 1988   823'.914   88–7440

ISBN 0-85640-409-8 (hardback)
0-85640-410-1 (paperback)

O land of password, handgrip, wink and nod,
Of open minds as open as a trap.

from 'Whatever You Say Say Nothing'
Seamus Heaney

to those who are
edged out of life

CONTENTS

PROLOGUE

Our story begins as James Gullion negotiates the road ramp in his beautifully blue Cortina. A British soldier with a red beret, irrelevant to our story, makes one appearance here; he gawks in through the car window at the two occupants and then, with smart military authority, signals the car to move on.

For Sarah, in the passenger seat, this is the second threshold she has crossed today. That morning she had already passed from the state of spinster to that of spouse and wife. Now she is passing from the South to the North of Ireland. She has yet to have all this newness consummated in ways she is not altogether clear about.

You see, Sarah was not what you would call 'superintelligent'. She might have scraped and slogged her way to a pass mark in her final BA examination (one of the proudest moments in her life, God love her) but she was, taking everything into consideration, dim.

Of course, a woman not blessed with the brain power of a genius can often advance herself if she but uses her charms to the fullest advantage. You understand what I mean. There are always enough men around who want nothing more than to suck the juices of the earth; and in their company such a woman may initially get away with murder, if she is also careful enough not to be murdered.

Well, as they say in pockets of the North, Sarah didn't have much fortune in her face. Her flesh was white and lifeless. She was thin. She wore appallingly thick spectacles. And her black hair (don't-stretch-your-imagination-Sarah) hung down either side of her face, as it had done when she was thirteen years old; its blackness only emphasising the white face. Needless to say, she never had sex. At college she was the kind of girl that boys could not conceive of as having anything more under her skirts than a dry old cobweb. The kind of girl who gets spoken to by men on the rare occasions when there is no other girl in the room.

These are cruel facts, but even at this stage, and after all that has happened, we owe it to Sarah to be truthful. Even when she was receiving her essay back in a tutorial group (a terribly pedantic and pretentious piece of garbage in three thousand words that the poor girl had spent four sunny weeks swotting through in the library while the rest of her classmates were swilling pints in the student bar), even then the professor was not above a touch of nasty sarcasm: 'Plod on, Sarah,' he said, 'plod on.'

And the other young assembled intelligences were not above a snigger or two; snivelling grovellers that they were, with their first-class honours.

Then she goes off and marries James Gullion. James Gullion from the North, as Ulster was affectionately described in Dublin. James Gullion, devout Catholic and brother to Joey the freedom fighter reportedly on the run for 'doing' a post office in the early days. That is to say, he blew the windows out of the post office prefab with a creamery can full of fertiliser. Joey – the runner Gullion, as they called him – the most wanted man in Casnagee.

Yes, married James Gullion, if you don't mind. And *devout* is a mild word for the religious soup on which James Gullion's mother reared her children. Not only did she have her husband's coffin draped with the Republican flag, for unspecified heroics in former days, but she had him togged out as well in a GAA football jersey before she nailed him in.

James did a part-time diploma course in agriculture at college, of which he was disproportionately proud, but for the most part he stayed at home to mind both the farm and the mother.

It was Marian that Sarah met first. She too was from Casnagee; a sullen pint-of-stout woman in the student bar who approached everything from Elizabethan poetry to trigonometry from the strict perspective of an Irish feminist. And to put it mildly, she

4

could be as cross as a bag of weasels. She always arrived in the bar with an entourage of bearded pot-bellied elder males, some over forty, who were known as the 'mature students' or the 'political crowd'. Marian took a shine to Sarah, brought her under her wing and introduced her to many of them, including the notorious Joey the Runner.

It was only much later that James made his quiet but persistent entrance on the scene. 'Quiet' does not fully cover James. He had the local parish priest, his mother and the cause of Irish freedom all wound into one solid icon that he was always and everywhere reverencing. It nurtured him, yet terrorised him. It sapped his will, stifled the breath of his imagination and left his soul no more than a frail leafless tree that you find stunted and wizened in the forest's shadows. James was no Clark Gable.

As to externals, he was a good block of a man, a respected fullback on the local football team. And after much methodical courting, marry Sarah he did.

It was also after an unholy row broke out between Mrs Gullion and the priest in Dublin, who did not agree with the use of two photographers on the altar and the fact that the musical ensemble from Casnagee only knew country-and-western songs for the service. Sarah would have been happy to side with the priest since it was her parish, but she was too nervous to get involved and in the end Mrs Gullion won. Not a good omen on the morning of Sarah's wedding. But the priest got what he considered his revenge by forgetting to turn on the heating in the church. It was the middle of January. Whatever discomfort that caused Mrs Gullion, it was nothing to the pain Sarah endured in her light cream bridal gown. As the organ was ready to bellow she looked more like someone dressed for the grave than for the wedding couch. Perhaps that too was unlucky.

A few photographs remain somewhere of that happy day. A handful of half-excited relatives and classmates standing on the steps of a church in Dublin, waving her farewell.

Yes, they waved her farewell as she crossed the threshold. Absence does not have a hearty effect on classmates. They simply forget. Sarah went to live up north somewhere. That's all. Some place called Casnagee. For all they knew, Casnagee didn't even exist.

But Casnagee existed all right. Locals said it came from the fact that along the lough shore the wind could change direction very suddenly. Less complimentary was the suggestion made sometimes by rival football teams that Casnagee meant 'turning with the wind' and that it reflected a ficklemindedness endemic to the people who lived there.

Casnagee was larger than a parish; it was an interlocking cluster of villages and townlands which snuggled in between hills and lakes in one of the remotest corners of Northern Ireland. A place where everyone was isolated; in little bungalows, old farmhouses or the public houses of the villages, they had all marked out for themselves relatively similar destinies – to look out the window at the house on the opposite hill was to look into a mirror. There were many lakes and waterlogged fields and open places where rushes grew, and ditches you could shelter in from a sudden rainstorm and long lanes with iron gates at every twist. And at the end of each long lane there was someone else who was exactly the same. To protect themselves then from this terrible awareness, people, as they say, kept to themselves. And from out of their isolation they paraded occasionally, for Sunday Mass or funerals, football matches or auctions, parish festivals and bazaars, or the parish liturgies of Holy Week.

Of course, that is not how James Gullion saw things as he drove up the long lane, opening and closing the iron gates. Nor is it what Sarah saw. At the end of the lane there was a new bungalow, sparkling white and fully furnished. Well it's not Castleknock, she admitted to herself, fingering the silver wedding presents already in place on the sideboard, but she could have done worse.

But then blink your eye, and years have passed. Years, and absolutely nothing has happened.

THE STORY

Joey was caught. They all drove to Dublin for the trial. A courtroom drama. And everyone who went up to Dublin for it wondered how long it would last. People wonder how long everything will last. People question the best day of the year; they ask – can it last?

The trial lasted two hours. Then it was over. Something was said about days of remission, which nobody understood. It sounded to Sarah like cancer. What had to be served was counted out.

When she thought of prison, she thought of breaking out; breaking out of prisons was necessary; everyone, she thought, should break out of prison. And the word *escape* follows the thought; to escape from something. She wondered had anyone ever escaped from anything. Was it right or proper that a person should escape? Her mother used to say you can never escape, especially when Sarah would get caught. The damage is done, her mother would say, you can't escape.

Sarah wondered a lot in the courtroom about the sexual life of the judge. Only vaguely did she hear something about the post office and the prison officers and a matter of the most serious nature. It's all adding up, she thought, but that was as close as she got to being aware of what might be going on. Anyway, who was she to ask questions?

The most dramatic moment in the courtroom was when everyone was saying the word *guilty*. Guilty. Guilty. And then, twelve something or other. Twelve wise men or twelve apostles or twelve members of the jury or twelve months or maybe twelve years.

'Jesus, Mary and Joseph,' she kept screaming in the corridor outside. 'Jesus, Mary and Joseph, they didn't give him twelve years did they? Did they? Will someone fucking tell me what's going on?'

But it was too late to be asking what was going on. She wouldn't be seeing Joey for a long time to come. And Joey used to be such fun. Used to brighten her up.

But then lots of people said that he couldn't be let to roam round the parish with a gun in his pocket. It's not what people find acceptable. He simply hasn't the right to blow up the post office. It costs thousands of pounds to fix and who pays for it? Exactly. In the heel of the reel people are happier with a bit of law and order. Somebody said that. When everything is rightfully measured out. The taxpayers are happier. And the priests get their dues.

People are constantly making a quick tot of something, on their feet as they go about the roads. Your brother might land in gaol for three or four or twelve years and you would be saying that it is short or long depending on how you felt about him. Or when a woman is not with a man, it seems to her like a long time, no matter what the tot. And life itself is short. For some it drags on and on.

There were other trials. In Dublin. In Belfast. In Omagh. In Derry. Trials every day of the week. It doesn't matter. Some people made a point of not going to them. Some people made a point of not going to Mass. That's the way things were. You see, one village was like any other. It was full of political boys and half the time you wouldn't know who you'd be talking to. Political boys anticipated everything and made the best of it. Political boys end up on top no matter what the circumstances of any particular village.

Sarah thought they were all the same. She tried to be herself. Her little life was divided into the 'first evening' and the 'second evening'. Every day was either the first day or the second day of something. And it went on and on like that as long as she could remember. Because people looked after her, it was always a struggle to come home to the village on her own. Someone would always be saying I'll take you home this evening, and she would be thinking – this is the second evening he took me home; I owe him something.

So down Joey went for twelve years. Hard to believe. But it happened to Marian too. Caught badly one time for drugs, and the baby was taken away by the father. That was tough.

Sarah herself would have liked to go away. She was ready for it. She had waited so long. She had even thought about the gun. But then she had wondered about Marian being so vitriolic sometimes. There was no question about what the outcome would be.

And then nobody ran for a good while, which was a bad sign in itself. The trials were running and signs were there, they told her, that things were getting hot. Things are hotting up, they'd say to her. Sarah was in a hot mood and she missed Joey's crack, and all she could do was think for hours about the boy in the grocery store. And she lived in the drawing room and had loads of time for that.

It must be five years since she had first come into that drawing room and looked at the silverware on the sideboard. He never came in there. He never came in there; it wasn't the custom, he said, in the country. She would sit in there on the sofa and listen to her old gramophone records. Not to worry that the stylus was worn or that the records were cracked and forever repeating. Sometimes he'd come in suddenly and switch it off. Why did he do that? Because he was worried or so he said. I could begin a new life, he would say. I could drop the gun. I wouldn't have to wait again for the sound of a car engine on the lane.

But all that blather made no difference. She knew that. Days often return to the night from where they originally emerged. One ends up back at the start. That's how she felt when he went on like that. Then he'd go out and get stone drunk. That way he did not notice the dark encroaching on him. He was not aware. Not being aware was the best method of defence. Everyone used it, especially in the court cases. When the prosecution hammered the defence with a battery of questions which all began with the words 'And is it not a fact', then the defence would bat each one back with the phrase 'I wasn't aware'.

Many times she found herself enquiring at the post office about what might be going on. Many times in the drawing room she would get to her feet, saying what is happening? even though there was nobody else there with her. She thought of her brain as a pillow of feathers in those days. Five years, she would say; five bloody years.

Others in the village tried to break down the isolation between them by saying over drinks: Oh, that's awful. That's terrible. That's inconceivable. Her heart would rise when she heard this, but she would add to herself that it was not their life so how could they know?

She argued with him. 'But he's your brother. I'm just fond of him.'

Both of them, then, would walk round the sofa in circles, as if trying to find each other, shouting all the while.

The word *suspended* had two associations for Sarah. Firstly, it was close to the idea of that belt she wore round her waist and from which hung four straps for the purpose of holding up her stockings. This was a thing she had done for no man, not even him, but only alone sometimes, before the mirror, attempting to break into some relationship with her self. The second association was of a man, himself in fact, naked and bound by hands and feet, dead, and suspended upside down from the ceiling of the garage. If she did that to him, then she might come into some relationship with his self. But if she did, she knew too that it would be over between them.

Long after she had sat down on the sofa and fallen into a dream, he still staggered round and round in a circle, as if he hadn't noticed her absence. The thought of him in the garage, suspended from the single rafter, and the sight of him staggering round the sofa, lecturing her, made her choke emotionally. And when she choked emotionally, her hands became as cold as ice.

Are you happy now? he would ask her defiantly, because it was clear to him that it was all and every way her fault. He could turn on her so easily. And she would nod as the space

12

between his face and hers narrowed, and then, because it was the thing to do, she would begin to cry. Sometimes the thought occurred to her that if God was a good judge, then he might intervene on such occasions. But nothing ever happened.

The first day was always the day of compromises. The second was the day for paying up. If only she could resist the first compromise, then the entire pattern of her life might change. This is my day, she would say to herself as it began, and fuck the easy options – it is my day and I'll do with it as I please.

What would Joey think if he thought you were buying suspender belts? He'd laugh, he would. Now what did you go and do a thing like that for? She could hear the voice ringing in the room but she was alone. That she knew, by looking around. By touching the four walls. She was alone. But his face is there. And his face is the colour of death. And his face wants her the fuck out of his house. He stands at the fireplace. His hands behind his back and his chest puffed up. Then she strips him, ties him and in seconds he is suspended upside down in the garage. And yet all the while she knows there is no one at all in the room.

Sarah stands against the wall so as to have the entire room in her view: the sofa, the fireplace, the gramophone and the dark table with the photographs. I have a life to live here, she tells herself. And I am legitimate. There is no reason in the world for me to hide. All this she says out loud to the empty room, as it is necessary for her to hear the words. I don't care who's in gaol, she screams, I am here, indefinitely.

By this time local opinion had it that Sarah was a bit of a cod. A bit of a weed. A bit too caught up in herself. They said she ought to get out more but then, when she joined the knitting circle, one woman claimed that Sarah pointed a needle at her one night with the intention of sticking it in her. They were losing their patience with Sarah.

In those villages there was an unusual texture to the word *glad*. It was used by political boys after a few drinks when they were discussing the downfall of some poor unfortunate who happened to be in the wrong place at the wrong time. I'm glad, they would say, their eyeballs full of lust. I'm just delighted.

What troubled Sarah the most was when people told her that it wasn't her house anyhow. I see, she would retort, I see. Good, they would say then, I'm glad you see.

In those villages there was never much meaning to the language used. Words were often no more than phonetic releases for a variety of energies and lust. Finding sense in such conversations was as difficult as finding the right townland when travelling to a funeral. It was as likely as not that you'd end up at the wrong funeral in the wrong town, and someone saying behind your back, you were hard enough to find when your mother was alive. Paper thin. Paper thin. That's all you're up to.

The nastiest thing that ever happened was when old Mrs Gullion, thin and breathless one winter with the flu, summoned Sarah and said, 'It's not your house and it never will be, so watch yourself.'

Sarah lost the cool. 'What the fuck do you want off me anyhow?' she screamed.

But the old woman smiled, told her to watch her language and then said, 'Get out.'

After that Sarah felt she had no reputation. Or to be more precise, she had a reputation. Mrs Gullion must have believed what they had said about herself and Joey. The rest of the parish must have believed it too, for one day a political boy was giving her a lift to Dublin and halfway there he stopped and asked her to do things which she had always thought degrading. Inside herself she was chasing round to catch the word *dignity* and pin it down so that the air of it would come out of her.

'No,' she said to him, 'please drive on.'

But he smiled and asked why. And then he said knowingly, 'It'll do no damage to your reputation.'

That sounded like he knew about something, though there

15

was nothing to know about; but she felt guilty anyhow.

The worst thing. The most degrading beyond anything she could ever have imagined, happened one night by the simple accident of leaving the bathroom door unlocked.

It was not uncommon for little boys to have piddle fights in the lavatory at the far end of the school yard. We all know that. This would happen as three or four boys were flowing up against the enamel, in a line, and suddenly one would turn round and skite the boy next to him. Thus causing all of them to turn hoses on one another and squeal so high that the teacher would come running from the other side of the playground, knowing that they were at it again. Boys will be boys and so forth. Each boy would claim victory, chanting I got Tommy, I got Tommy, or, I got Brady, I got Brady. And of course, all of them would be saturated in urine.

But Sarah found it more than uncommon for a man fully grown into adulthood to even conceive of, let alone gain satisfaction from, the act of urinating over another human being.

But it was herself she blamed. After all, she would say to herself, what sort of animal am I to let him do that? For years she remembered it. He had done it while she was in the bath, and she had wept uncontrollably and then sat there, naked, biting her thumb, allowing it to go cold all over her as he put the kettle on in the kitchen. Her clearest thought at that moment had been that it was rarely she had heard him making tea. But afterwards she would often think she deserved all she got, after she allowed him to do that. There was something in her she did not quite understand from that night on. There was a stain there all the time.

Marian. Remember Marian? Well, she was back in Casnagee by now too, always orbiting the white bungalow of James Gullion. She argued against acceptance of anything. But she was so strong and uncontrollable in her rages that Sarah was either too ashamed or too frightened to mention the incident to her.

Marian had height and strength. She could lean against the Regency writing desk and give out to everyone. Marian never had kidney infections. Marian was one of those warrior-women you worshipped from a distance, but to whom you mentioned very little. It was too terrible to expose yourself to a strong person.

Marian used to wave her handkerchief about in front of her when she was talking. And she never whinged, no matter what the problem. Marian was definitely against whinging. Nor was she ever ashamed. If she was menstruating, she said so – even to the barman. She could cut the socks from under a mule. Stifled nothing. An enormous heavy woman by now, she created her own order about her wherever she went and fitted people into it; she was so well-built that she met with few arguments. Brought people under her jurisdiction and showed no mercy to the wicked.

And oh, did Sarah love her for that. Marian was her champion. If only she could be around all the time.

There is a difference between isolation and privacy. In those villages and up the long lanes in the hills between one village and another there was no privacy. A knock on the door could be anyone. And they'd walk in. So that people were never done knocking on each other for information.

A knock on the door could mean the creamery man or the travelling shop or the Artificial Insemination Man. Then there were men always calling about double glazing for the windows. Sarah always made sure that the windows were thoroughly clean, so that not even Mrs Gullion could catch her off guard. Catch her unawares and make some cutting remark about the state of the place. And if the double-glazing man came, she would say thank you very much but I like them as they are, and it would be obvious to him and all the world that she kept her windows clean. That would be one moment when she could say that reality matched the spoken word. But if only a knock on the door could always mean Marian.

And funny enough, there were things in the same district that were never clean. Like a man's hands, or the old brown coat he might use when foddering cattle in winter – that was always damp and smelly and hung on the back door. Other things were attended to with meticulous devotion. The bath, for instance, each time the man left it, was attacked with scouring cream by the woman of the house. Sarah always tried to think nice thoughts about her man when she did it, and she did it every single day of her life. Not that he bathed that often, but it passed half an hour. And it was truly remarkable how many bungalows, houses or cottages you could enter and find the rim of the toilet seat wet from where the last man had pissed.

One day Marian had said in a conciliatory tone, 'Well, at least he's clean.'

'Why do you say that?' enquired Sarah.

'Because,' said Marian, 'the toilet seat is always dry.'

Marian would put her chin in her hand and lean over the kitchen table and talk about men being trained to mind babies. The presence of that grin helped Sarah eat. If she woke up in the morning and thought about Marian's face, she would say to herself today I'm going to eat a lot. And mostly this came to be true.

But sometimes Marian too began to eat the face off her.

I warned you, she'd say.

You gave me your word, she'd say.

Even when she was alone, Sarah was still hearing this voice and pulling the bedcovers up over her face. I'm sorry, she would say back to the empty room, I'm sorry, OK?

If only she could go to the seaside with her. Her and Marian. Why not? They could link arms together and rub noses and walk along the beach in woollen caps with tassels, and anoraks shielding them from the long wind.

But Marian was screaming at her.

What age is he?

What age are you?

On and on like that until it no longer mattered. Sarah wanted to say you're not being fair, but she knew that if she did, then Marian would say she was only whinging.

What age is he?

What age am I?

What age are you?

Screaming she was.

'Look,' she said, 'there was seven brothers, and me.' But she stopped and looked directly at Sarah, as if she were going to say something else and then wouldn't.

It was very strange, Sarah thought, very strange to be fighting like this. But whatever they had been talking about, and Sarah could not remember an hour later, they never mentioned it again.

But perhaps it is better to pause here for a moment and leave aside the descending spiral in order to open the door to another character.

Sarah could not say exactly when Doctor Murray had entered her life. In fact sometimes she could not tell if it was March or April. White-faced as ever, long streaks of grey already appearing in her hair and, most upsetting of all to her, a thin line of black hair on her upper lip, she just blinked her way through the years in a continual state of shock. Why Doctor Murray entered is also difficult to say. Certainly it was nothing important. More a question of minor headaches, sores and pains, sleepless nights and the common cold. But gradually he had positioned himself on the stage, like a prop or a piece of the scenery.

The door opens and enter Doctor Murray. He is entering his own house and he reminds himself that it is his own house. Most gratifying. After all, he had gone to college. He was a competent professional man. His graduation photograph hung on the wall of the dining room. Doctor Murray often looked at that photograph. He often made a point of making straight for it once he entered the house. He was home then.

He had no curls left – far from it, he was as bald as an egg. And he was slightly more rotund now; in fact, he was as round as an egg. Ah, yes yes, but, he would say to the photograph, we're not men of the flesh. This curious remark meant that his ego was in no way shaken by being small, fat and bald. No, he would say, leave the flesh to those who take exercise. (And you can well guess what Doctor Murray's opinion of joggers was.)

Nor was the good doctor much for conversation. In fact, he dreaded having to share meals with anyone. It was always easier to stretch than to be saying pass-the-marmalade-please-thank-you and pass-the-butter-please-thank-you, every second minute. And when putting them on with a knife, the toast made a crackle which reflected some quaint inefficiency in his character, or so he thought, and he was loath to display it in company. Marmalade often dribbled down the side of the jar and then his finger got sticky and stuck to everything else; aaah Jesus Christ, he'd hiss, an expression of frustration unbecoming for a man of his dignity to be heard to utter in the dining room, by strangers. Strangers or family, what's the difference? There was no difference to the doctor.

The point was that to have anyone assert that he messed the marmalade (never mind that as a child he got irritated by it to boot) was intolerable. For it to be said that he soiled the table-cloth? Goodness. And right in front of her, the slut, the little hussy, whoever she is.

But who is she? Mothers, maids, they're all the one, Doctor Murray would mutter. Aye, maids and mothers.

Doctor Murray didn't mind not being perfect, as long as no one knew. He could bump into things as often as he liked, alone, and curse the chair that bruised his bare foot; but never in public.

The village was so nervous of him that they could do or say very little in his company. A silence that, on social occasions, he understood to imply respect. But the more he sheltered his own inadequacies the more nervous people became, resulting in a devastating decline in his surgeries and clinics. Only a few who had known him over thirty years as the family doctor remained loyal. (Such was the case with Mrs Gullion, who wouldn't hear tell of anyone else being called if ever James or Sarah took to the bed with flu.) People simply found it difficult to admit any illness in front of him, and as his practice dwindled he came to the opinion that there was too little poor health in the community. That people went to other doctors or hospitals and died regularly did not strike him as being at variance with his theory. People about here, he would say, leaning against the bar in the local hotel as was his wont, are a healthy lot; all the hard work and clean living.

Well, the wee girl behind the counter was hardly going to contradict him there. Although her youthful intuition was capable of putting all the complexities of Doctor Murray's psychological disposition in one little nutshell, when she said once to her mammy: 'Jeez, that Doctor Murray fella is fierce odd.'

But in general the people of those villages did not think very often about Doctor Murray. Like the old red telephone kiosk outside the post office, which had survived world war, civil war and even Joey the Runner's post-office bomb, Doctor Murray was part of the scenery.

Plenty of women had babies without him. There was always the chemist. And the grocer. Yes, and the grocer's wife, who they said was gifted. Though no one ever spoke about it publicly. One presumed people wished the doctor well and asked no questions about what went on in his house. If you get what I mean. Was it anyone's business what went on behind closed doors? No sir, it was not. That was the verdict of every woman who ever went to morning Mass of a weekday. Nobody's business.

A woman's business was to make sure she had a pair of everything in the hot-press and after that, ask no questions about your neighbour. That's what they said. On the steps of the chapel. In the name of the Father and of the Son and of the Holy. . . Holy what? Holy Spirit, that's the good wee *gasún*.

And so we return to that descending spiral in which Sarah found herself, out of control and helter-skeltering. The bungalow was a foreign land and her husband, after their prosaic and passionless courtship, had returned his attentions to more solid, but equally passionless, matters: the care of the farm and two bungalows. His mother lived half a mile away and yes, you can guess, in a little white bungalow built on the site of the old farmhouse which had deteriorated rapidly after Mr Gullion's death. Sarah discovered her husband had a bad temper and that the soft-spoken, gentle country giant had a dark side in private. But what's new? She could have taken that – many women had to. And she was familiar with that profound axiom which the world fastens to the bedpost of such women: you made your bed, you can lie in it. She had no pity for herself on that account. But she was frightened by a strange sense of numbness; a feeling that the world around her didn't exist.

Summertime wasn't easy for her. From her window she could see the lake's shoreline, the picnic area, the cluttered cars from the city. She was living in a land dotted with 'scenic spots' which the city folk sought out on Sunday afternoons and bank holiday weekends. They came in all colours of saloon cars, and walked about the grass verge or sat on deck chairs beside their cars, eating sandwiches and drinking flasks of tea. Their children would play beside the water in swimming togs, and sea gulls, yes sea gulls, would hover and pick at the scraps of bread crust which they discarded. Then suddenly the wind of Casnagee would rise from the lake without warning and spoil everything. It's cold, Mammy, the little boys and girls would say; and Daddy would survey the scene and announce judiciously that it was time to go back.

That moment when they were all gone and the shoreline was again deserted and the hill fields became choked with the shadow of brooding clouds, was a moment of intense nostalgia for Sarah.

And then Marian always said you should never go back. But what did that mean? After all, Marian had thrown up the husband, lost the baby in a court case and returned to Casnagee to start an organic farm. Surely that was going back. Sarah was too timid or afraid to tell Marian that she didn't understand the half of what she talked about.

'It all feels so empty sometimes,' Sarah said once.

'Ah, that's the emigration,' Marian explained, with a wave of her hand.

You see, there was a lot of emigration from those villages and it was a subject before everyone's mind. The opinion of the hotel keeper was that those who had left and gone across the sea would never come back.

'I have a nephew over there.' he said. 'I get letters all the time.' (At this point he would reach for the airmail envelope behind the beer bottles.) 'Oh, he's over there this five years. Never coming back. Sure why would he? Eh? Why would he?'

The hotel keeper felt validated because one of his own had made the break with Ireland. He may never have crossed the border himself but, by association, he was an exile. And of course, everyone knew that in those villages there were only the dregs left. The pubs were quieter, if not empty.

The dregs spent their dole money in public houses, tormenting themselves with fanciful notions of what it must be like 'out foreign'. They had a vision of bright young people in yellow tee shirts on tropical beaches and they were haunted by it. Especially when it was pissing rain and windy outside the door.

Jeez, someone would say finally, it's fucking awful weather for this time of year.

Ah, but sure yis are always complaining, retorts the hotel keeper. Always complaining. And complaining never got anyone anywhere. (O-ho, he thought to himself, rub them in it.)

Nor was the winter any easier for Sarah. Less happened. At Hallowe'en a few children might run round the wet laneways in ghost-filled sheets, looking for coppers. Sarah turned all the lights out that evening and sat in the dark so that they would think there was no one at home. The sound of their little shoes would be followed by a knock and a rhyme or two, or a tune on the tin whistle, and finally, a few ripe curses as they realised that she was inside but had the lights off because she did not intend answering the door.

Jeez, then someone would say across the counter at the hotel, you won't find it now till Christmas.

But Christmas seemed to be just one more obstacle in life to be got over by everyone; its imminence caused nothing but worry. And we are not talking here about one year or two or three. But a pattern, a never-ending cycle; a treadmill of existence.

No, thought Sarah, this can't be real.

Doctor Murray was a great man for his gin in the hotel. Philosophising to himself at the bar. I think, he'd say, things are getting worse. Whether he meant the weather or the political situation, no one was quite sure. Maybe he meant the condition of his liver under the strain of seven double gins, for the more he drank the more he issued his gentle refrain.

One night he called the girl behind the counter to him with his wiggling finger. She approached. He put his hand on her shoulder and pulled her slightly over the counter and said with great sincerity into her ear: 'Do you know that you can measure any man, any man, by how he takes the top off his boiled egg.'

This was an insight the young lady was not enriched by because her attention was directly afterwards drawn to the floor. Doctor Murray's hand, as it returned to his side having released the young girl's shoulder, cleaned two pints of ale and a mineral from the counter. And in the crash of glass about the place the young lady completely forgot what he was saying about boiled eggs.

That hotel lounge did good business on the weekends during the winter. Young girls dressed in black skirts; girls with per-fumes. But good girls. Oh yes, country girls, who might paint their eyes and dress in black leather on a Friday night, but country girls, you could leave to mind a child and not worry. Dizzy little girls from secondary school convents. Marian didn't mind them but they frightened the life out of Sarah. If ever she went there, she always went to the toilet first to talk at herself in the mirror. I'll have a gin-and-tonic, she would say. Yes. Just one gin-and-tonic. That's no harm. But the girls would be stretching and reclining like young kittens, tossing their hair this way and that and making shapes with their lips and sticking out their tongues, so that the doctor in his black Crombie and white scarf would get magnificently plastered at the bar, and his eye through the mirror behind the bar lapping them up, until they were all giggling behind their hands and saying – hello, doctor – every time they went up to order another drink.

'Ah for goodness' sake,' Marian said, 'don't be so paranoid. Sure I'm related to the half of them. They're only kids.'

But Sarah, for some reason, had got the impression that they were laughing at her and based on that false assumption, she had considerably more than one gin-and-tonic.

But a woman can't go on indefinitely in a world that doesn't exist. Sarah eventually found her own company. She was sitting on the bed one morning, in those black exotic laces and straps. The accoutrements of her solitary pleasure. But she was staring in the bedroom mirror and weeping over her white little body when in the mirror, behind her, there appeared to her the extraordinarily compassionate face of Christ.

Sarah, he said to her. *Sarah*.

Through the glass in the mirror their eyes met.

Sarah, he said.

A word her husband had seldom used in five years.

The humiliation that Sarah received at the hands of her husband can only be guessed at. There were things she said. There was the way she behaved at times. It all added up to something. When you arrived in her home, the clues were all about the place. You could almost sense him still in the house. Sarah would breathe out blue smoke into the drawing room air, if you asked her about it, and be silent. That said everything.

Marian was no fool. She fished and fished till it came out. She knew how to throw the right question into the air and let it hang there; like, has it started again? Marian said she was ready to intervene, any time Sarah said so. She sealed the promise with a warm kiss on the cheek. She offered to stay the night. But no. Sarah would insist on her leaving before he got back.

'He'll go spare if he finds you here,' Sarah said.

'Well at least,' said Marian, 'phone me if it starts again. I can drive round. It'd be no trouble at all.'

For a while then Sarah thought of Marian and Christ as the same person. She was tall and holy. Except that Marian always got into her car at the end of every conversation and drove off down the lane. Sarah would return to the drawing room and stare out the window, thinking to herself that years ago she would never even have believed anything like this. She didn't think there was anywhere in the country as remote as Casnagee. Its remoteness had been its beauty when she came first. She had looked at the bungalow with amazement.

'That's for you,' he had said.

But it wasn't. It was his and now she was his. And he was never at home. She gazed out the window until the moon was a ghost, so high up that it reflected in the lake down below her.

When she walked with her new husband on the streets of the village, he would insist on linking arms with her. Then, with subtlety, he could convey to her through this contact when to stop or start, just like a dog. He stopped at the shoe shop. He was looking at shoes. He stopped at the newspaper shop to speak with Peter McDonagh. This linking of arms made her want to screech. Like a dog on a leash.

Oh he was the boss all right. There was no doubt about that. And the clothes she wore were his, because he paid for them. Only what was hidden from him was her own. Her lingerie, purchased whenever she got a chance to visit Dublin. She had a drawer full of white and black lace. Beautiful things bought in swanky shops, though even when she was buying them, she would look around and see men at the counter for their girl-friends and it made her feel like a widow.

And could she do anything about it? Not a bloody thing. Get a few tablets from Doctor Murray perhaps. Tipple at the gin. Or turn on the women's programme on the radio to discover that whatever was troubling her, whatever was wrong with her, wasn't even unique. Women didn't exist as individuals. Up and down the island, in towns, cities, and countryside; in corpora-tion flats and detached suburban utility rooms women were scraping the walls. A hidden whinging shadow in the corner of someone else's room. And those who had used seduction, assert-iveness and cunning to be the authors of their own lives, were made social outcasts; labelled as cantankerous wasps. No, how could Sarah change her life when a whole society was paralysed? And this was the pain that went to the very centre. It wasn't that he abused her. It wasn't that he didn't love her or that she cleaved to him. It was more that women didn't exist as individuals. They were all having exactly the same things happen to them. Sarah's life was a cliché. She wasn't unique, and if she wasn't unique, then it was her who didn't exist and not the world around her.

Try explaining that to Doctor Murray. Poor Sarah did once, though she got no further than a few inarticulate phrases before he told her that it was undoubtedly a touch of the woman's thing and flung her out with a bottle of sedatives.

28

Sarah cried so often now that Mrs Gullion said, with agrarian acid, she must have her bladder behind her eyeballs. An unfortunate phrase, considering what was so soon afterwards to develop out of Sarah's bladder.

But first a slight digression. Timely and discreet reference can now be made to that which was never referred to in front of Sarah: politics. Of course it was going on all the time. But you don't see anything, do you? So what's there to talk about?

Sarah's first encounter with local politics was sudden and shocking. They had someone in the shed at the other end of the back yard. A young fellow. She could hear him howling. They were all in there – her husband and, to be discreet, 'the other men'. She slipped across under the moon and peeped in a side window. By the golden light of a Tilley lamp she could see them beating him. He was lying on the ground, a hood over his head, the rest of his body naked. His wrists and ankles tied. Long shafts of fog billowed down her nostrils into the night air. She watched on.

And she was aware of being very excited. Frightened and confused, yes. But something both terrible and significant was happening and she was witnessing it. The men kept shouting at the boy on the floor and he pleaded with them. Then it all stopped. The men were parleying. The boy, shivering. Sarah thought his rump was like a horse and she whispered to herself, you wouldn't do that to a horse.

What they were doing in there made no sense to her. She returned to the kitchen and opened the window and continued listening to the squeals of the young fellow drifting over the yard under the moonlight. It was like a night a cow might calf, and it was romantic.

When her husband finally came in, he stood at the kitchen table, with his hands in his pockets, smiling at her, as if he knew she had heard them and was glad. There was a strange glow in his expression. She found it impossible to say anything.

'Make us a cup of tea,' he said at last, 'I need it.' And he actually smiled at her. Then he poured whiskey into the cup and almost immediately wanted to go to bed and ride her. That was the only word he used for their intimate moments.

But there is no explaining some quirks in human nature, for at that moment she delighted in the strange perversion of obedience and submission to him; taking his trousers off in the bedroom and kissing as she did so, his rump, and later, squeezing her fingers into the flesh of his cheeks and thinking of horses.

Marian said she was crazy. Marian's big blue eyes could flash all over the room when she was enraged. And then she could be soft and put her arms round Sarah, as gentle as a nun, and say, oh Sarah, what are we going to do with you at all? Sarah would press her face against the other woman's shoulder and breathe like a machine gun, as if she were on the verge of tears. Marian hoped she would break. But she didn't. She was resisting Marian. She had her own company now.

Sarah often noticed as she was putting a kettle on in the kitchen that her fingertips were blue. They weren't always blue, she thought, and it couldn't just be the cold. For the kitchen was warm. The range was lighting. But she had developed the habit of putting her hands round the kettle to warm them. She talked to the kettle and the coal scuttle and the mirror and the drawer with the lace and, all the time, of course, to herself. But even when the house was empty, she always spoke in whispers. Even with Marian she spoke in whispers.

'Well,' Marian said one day, 'did you ask him?'

Sarah said she hadn't. She had been afraid of asking about going off with Marian, just the two of them, for a fortnight. It would only have caused a storm.

'So you didn't ask him?'

'No.'

'And that's all?'

Yes, that was all.

Suddenly she found words. 'Marian,' she said, 'you get what you deserve in life and you have to take what you get. Even if it gets up your nose.'

Marian was baffled. 'He's playing with fire,' she said.

But Sarah laughed and said, 'Marian, he's a teaspoon. And I need him.'

At first Sarah did not realise it was a kidney infection. All she knew was that the bed was damp and he was shouting at the top of his lungs and going lunatic around the bedroom. He went out and took a bath, dressed in silence and, for the first time in his life, left the house without breakfast. Sarah lay on until eleven o'clock, listening to the magazine programme on the radio. She wondered did even the man on the radio care about her, chirping away in the radio, happy as Larry with himself as she lay there stinking.

I'm in for it now, she thought. Things will be rough. I've done it now. I've done it. This is the final blow. He'll be able to show his displeasure with abandon.

Mrs Gullion's clothes were always washed by Sarah. Sarah had the tumble drier. So there was always a shelf of Mrs Gullion's things in the hot-press. To punish herself, Sarah now burrowed for them and after bathing, she dressed herself in that woman's clothes. The thought of those clothes on her sent shivers through her body. But she must. She must. Then she gathered up the soiled sheets, taking her time and sparing herself nothing as she touched them. The mattress she flung up on its side against a one-bar heater.

To appreciate how swiftly Sarah was helter-skeltering into despair, it is necessary to observe her at the tumble drier – a wooden thing wearing her mother-in-law's dressing gown, a slight tremble in her lower lip and her head swilling with every failure, every inadequacy, every foolish mistake in class, that memory could fling up at her. It all twirled around in her like the clothes in the machine. And all because she had, at almost thirty years of age, pissed in the bed. Did the possibility of illness occur to her? Life is not that kind. She stood like a little girl, bowed and ready for her punishment. If only she could rinse herself with some lethal detergent.

Her husband never opened his mouth to her until the following morning. 'What in the name of Jeezis started that?' he asked.

'I know, I know,' she replied. 'I'm sorry. I don't know what happened.'

He must have thought that was taking it a bit lightly, for he had one of, what she called, his flips. 'I know fucking well what happened,' he lashed back. 'Bone lazy. Bone fuckin' lazy.'

His mother arrived in the afternoon with a set of clean sheets. She told Sarah to throw out the other ones. Sarah thought that was ridiculous but, 'Throw them out,' said the mother, 'they'll only be upsetting him.'

The washing machine wasn't turned off for a long time. You see, as if to underline the relentless cruelty of life, it happened again. And again. Sarah tried everything. Five pairs of cotton pyjamas. But she could feel it inside her. She knew it would happen again. And it did. Yet again.

'That's final,' he said, 'make up the bed for yourself in the spare room. The house stinks.'

His mother arrived again. This time with a rubber sheet and an enormous expression of disgust on her thin little face. She wouldn't even stop for a cup of tea. 'I think, dear,' she said, 'you ought to see Doctor Murray.'

Well, that's how the 'thing', as she later called it, happened. He must have gone to his mother's for the dinner that day, for she didn't see him till after midnight. She was beginning to notice a pain in her kidney and thought a hot bath would relax her and contribute to a dry night. He was drunk and had entered the bathroom before realising she was there. He stood for a second at the toilet bowl, about to release himself, and then he burst out laughing.

'How ya now?' he said turning to her, still laughing.

At first she thought he was just in good form, remembering the last joke from the pub. Then the smile went from his face like snow off a rope.

'Do ye know what ye might need?' he said in a tone of mocking intimacy. 'A taste of yer own medicine.' Then he burst out laughing again as he poured himself in a large comical arc into the bath water instead of the toilet bowl.

A joke, he insisted. Just a little joke. You see, when some men have the drop of drink taken, he explained. And as he admitted, he had a fair bit in him that night. That would have been obvious to Sarah, to judge by the measure he succeeded in splattering into the bath.

All the girls rallied after that. Marian organised it. The long winter days were spent with Sarah, staring at the range, saying that the spring was only around the corner. They would stare at his damp coat on the back door or at his boots under the sink, as if they were observing the track of a strange beast. There was Mary and Nora and Louise, and they all came on different afternoons and did their best. Marian, head and shoulders above them all, would orchestrate the conversation, pulling everyone into it, and as they said, pulling Sarah out of herself.

But often it appeared as if Sarah had gone too far. She would look around the room and the girls were strangers to her. Who were they anyhow? Then she would close her eyes, open them again, and they were gone. Vanished. In their place was her husband, his arse to the heat of the range, stroking his temple and saying he would insist on her seeing the doctor. Sometimes he would stare at her for ages, without a word, and then shrug his shoulders and say it was a joke. Just a joke.

And finally, when it had all been arranged, she told herself that it was no big deal. Yes, she accepted in herself that she had to go. Plenty of people get taken away to hospital and people pass no remarks. You put on your clothes one day, more cheerful than before, and there's no need for explanations. A leather suitcase. A peck on the cheek for those lined up at the door to see you off. Hospitals are hospitals, even lunatic asylums.

A big clock in the hall hammering the time away. Maybe she should kiss that goodbye because it might be the only thing in her life that never gave out to her. And so while they all stand around, all the relatives and the girls, and Marian, and him, and all full of their own conceit because they all think they are the special one she will miss, it is in fact a clock to which she is secretly bidding farewell and not them at all.

Marian drove. Marian was the one for that. And before the car was down to the end of the lane he had the door closed.

'Well,' he said, going into the kitchen, 'that's that.'

'Are they gone?' his mother asked. She was making him a cup of tea.

A digression? No. Just the memories that rinsed and rinsed around in Sarah's head as Marian held the wheel and the little Renault 4 bounced along the roads towards the psychiatric hospital. Marian gripped the wheel rather tight, for she had not been spared from just a tinge of despair herself. She knew, for instance, that Sarah's mother had ended badly, in the mad house.

Long long ago a letter had come for Sarah. It was from her mother and it upset her deeply. It was lunch time and that morning the hospital had phoned to say her mother had died during the night. For a while she was angry with her mother for having the sinister nerve to speak to her from the grave – this was how she understood the letter.

And she was disappointed too when she opened it to find that far from being a revelation of anything important from her mother's deathbed, it was full of old nonsense, which indicated that her mother was tasting as little of death as she had of life. Sarah was only seventeen when her mother went off with the fairies and had to be put away. The letter said that the coloured paper was lovely and that the nuns were very good. 'Always say your prayers, Sarah, and I'll see you on Sunday, please God.'

Her mother had told her once, before going into the hospital and when Sarah was very young, never to chase after the boys. Let them do all the chasing, she would say.

Sarah spent as long as she could being a little girl, spending time with her mother. Then she decided to leave and her mother never gave her any advice again. When Sarah went home for visits at the weekend, all her mother would talk of was God and how he'd be calling her soon enough. He called her six months later, but just to the hospital. Was that Sarah's fault? Of course not, but you know what children are like.

She had just finished college when the letter came. It took her the following year to sort out everything, emotionally. It was like an explosion inside her; physically and mentally she went haywire. She drifted from one thing to another and couldn't concentrate. Her bedsit in Ranelagh became a jumbled pile of bad odours. God, heretofore not central in her life, became her enemy. It's your fault, she would say, passing the church door. Her fireplace filled up with empty cigarette packets and dozens, perhaps hundreds, of fag ends. Nothing disgusted her more than to see cigarette ends lying in the fireplace or on saucers. Yet she hadn't a clean saucer in the house.

She just allowed things to happen. As she allowed him to court her in the National Ballroom on Wednesday and Friday nights. As she allowed him to go further and further until he had the ring on her finger, the arrangements made and the bungalow purchased, as he said himself.

He lured her with an entire universe of villages and farms, and doctors and nurses and mammies and daddies. It was like a soap opera coming to life; and sitting on a bed in Ranelagh, sharing the toilet with six other flats and thinking about the little graveyard her mother was so recently folded into, his offer was not unattractive.

But he hadn't offered himself. As Marian drove through crossroads and round roundabouts Sarah was staring out the window at the ghostly leafless trees that stood out in the fog of the fields and thinking, no, he never offered himself.

Snow fell. James Gullion was crucified trying to fodder cattle in it. And there were other things annoying him. Letters received that he made no comment on. Political things.

There were certain letters people received that they read and tore up. Then they would burn all the little pieces in the fireplace immediately. It was coming towards Christmas and for some reason people were getting edgy. Political things.

Getting very nervous. Drifts of snow mounted in slopes against the walls of fields and gardens.

The stumped fingers of the rose shrubs in the doctor's lawn were barely visible. Every branch of the doctor's cherry tree was topped with a line of snow. People were never done haggling about turkeys on the street beside red Ford Escort vans. People were buying and selling turkeys at a fierce rate. Everybody had resolved, and were grimly determined, to have a happy Christmas.

Without putting a tooth in it, they were all, except Marian, reasonably happy and satisfied that Sarah had been put away. With what passed for compassion in that place, they said on the steps of the chapel going in to midnight Mass that sure it was the nerves. And it was him they felt most sorry for. Sure he must have had an awful time of it altogether. Women were capable of being the most conclusive about the matter: sure, they said, wasn't she always dirty.

Sarah spent Christmas Day watching television in the patients' common room.

And there's not a lot can be said for the television on Christmas Day. 'On Christmas Day all Christians sing, to hear the news the angels bring.' Bumpety bumpety bump. Even the jingles for the test cards are made out of carols. Snow falling on a Christmas pudding. And *The Wizard of Oz*. So that's where Sarah spent the day. In the common room. The other patients, male and female, in dressing gowns, flexed into armchairs around the walls, smoking like chimneys.

A trolley of Christmas cake. A yoke for making cocoa in the kitchen. And a Christmas tree in the corridor with a few silver streamers hanging off it and a red paper star on top.

'Do you ever feel like an intruder sometimes?' she asked a nurse, and the nurse smiled at her and rubbed a hand across Sarah's brow.

In her head Sarah knew what she wanted to say. She wanted to say that she felt like an intruder in the world. That she had sort of slipped in unnoticed and ought not to be there.

'Especially today,' she persisted to the nurse. 'Especially today.' Her fingers were fumbling with pieces of broken icing on a plate. 'I think,' she said, 'it's tomorrow.'

'Yes,' the nurse said, holding her hand, 'it's tomorrow.'

By the time Marian arrived, Sarah had ceased to think about herself. She was aware of the other patients. There was a man who kept shouting in the corridor. And the young boys in choral dress singing on the television were so pretty that she wanted to interfere with them. And when they sang 'Silent Night', she cried. When Marian walked up to her, Sarah didn't recognise her. Then she took Marian's hand in hers and placed it inside her pyjamas and stroked herself with Marian's hand,

40

and the tears flooded down her face.

'Oh pet,' Marion said, and embraced her.

There was always a fog hanging round the hospital. And there were signposts in the gardens that she found difficult to read. And she could never hear any birds. And the ambulances were always ticking over, wasting petrol. And the doctors had big cars: Renault 20s and Volvos. And there was an elderly woman in a blue housecoat who dominated the reception area. And a telephone was always ringing in the corridor. That was about it. Marian could get no sense out of her beyond that.

'Well of course,' the nurse explained, 'she's on medication.'

But the fact was that Sarah had discovered her own company. No one was more important to her at that time than Christ, whose photograph she kept in the breast pocket of her dressing gown. He was always with her. None of them could see that. All they could see was that Sarah was drifting further and further out to sea; further away from them.

Sarah couldn't see much either. A glass door; a long line of beds; a smell of failure hanging over the green linoleum. Jesus. Jars of sweets. Chairs of wicker and lockers beside each bed. Bald heads and sunken eyes. A man smoking a cigar. A man in the corridor waving his hands and preaching gobbledegook at the visitors.

'Don't pull up that screen, sister. Don't surround my bed. I want to see. Give me my glasses back, please, sister.'

But they took the screens away again when the examination was over. Returned her possessions. New starched sheets.

And there, at the foot of the bed, was the beautiful face of Christ whispering *Sarah*.

A nurse was putting a hand to her forehead and checking her temperature.

'Will I be all right, sister?' she enquired.

'Of course you will.'

Christ nodded too.

'But why would I piddle in the bed,' Sarah asked the nurse, 'when the floor is in front of me?'

'That's right,' the nurse said, 'that's right.'

There was one nurse who wore a particularly soft pair of white shoes. Like slippers. They were silent on the floor and Sarah's heart always sank when she saw them walk down the corridor in the evenings on the way home. I'm off now, the nurse would say. See you all in the morning.

Sarah's heart would sink right down.

But psychiatric hospitals are not what they used to be. Admission to such institutions is not a final comment on anybody. People are encouraged to come and go, to adjust at community level, to cope with the world outside.

Sarah could hardly have been there more than a week. The first time. Patients came and went. Sarah was, as the people of Casnagee remarked, in and out of the 'mental' all the time. And who would pay the slightest heed to that? No one at all. Trouble with the nerves was as common as the flu.

But now suddenly it is March and the days are getting brighter. Early sun and cloudless skies and a sharp wind. The tops of the houses and the cars are glistening.

He is walking down the road. He is lifting planks of wood off a lorry. He is standing in the timberyard. And in the shop beside that timberyard an elderly lady is checking the delivery slips.

Sarah is familiar with that shop. That timberyard. Women know when a breadvan is coming, she tells herself. I could have told her that a breadvan was coming. Women know these things instinctively. In fact, anyone in the village would know that the breadvan was coming. It was time for it to come. It always came at the same time every day. Otherwise how could they eat?

And if only she could be out by the lake shore with Jesus this morning. But she must wait till Jesus is ready for her. Jesus loves her, you see. Not like the women in the village – they hate her. And the man in the red-and-white breadvan hates her. That poor man delivering bread. So bereft of any love to give anyone. She could see that in his eyes.

Do you think Joey is sorry now? she asks Jesus, but Jesus doesn't answer. Aah, look, there's the school bus coming down the street. It parks outside the school, waiting for the children and the bare trees cast a sort of dappled shadow over it. Lovely, like lace.

What time did Doctor Murray want to see her at? Oh yes, ten o'clock. Ten o'clock, just in time. Well hey ho, down the street, off to see the doctor. And the bus across the road there, waiting to bring the children to the swimming pool.

It was just about the time the breadman came. It was the day Sarah went for her weekly to Doctor Murray. Tablets and things. She was, in fact, inside his gate, admiring the early blossoms on the cherry tree.

Jesus was standing beside her and he said, *It makes you think of Joey, doesn't it?*

She nodded.

The breadvan just sat there.

That's the van, she said.

Yes, Jesus answered her, *I know.*

For there were men who had been standing at the door all night. There were those who knew and those who were nervous. Political things. There were villagers still in their bare feet squinting out the windows at the street. At Sarah standing in the doctor's garden, and at the red-and-white breadvan, and at the school bus further down under the trees.

There were a lot of political boys that morning making important telephone calls. Nervous, edgy telephone calls; dialling, listening and putting the receiver down again.

Before Sarah has reached the porch, the doctor is already opening the door. Is he going for the morning paper? Perhaps. The breadvan is pulling out. But look, a blue car is pulling in. And there, two old ladies with old-fashioned hats and prayer books processing along on the footpath. Are they on their way to Mass? Perhaps. What a beautiful morning it all is. It is on a morning like this that Jesus will finally be ready for her.

But the blue car bumps into the nose of the van. Dear oh dear, what a silly thing to do. And the driver of the van is talking out the window. And then from nowhere there is a man with a gun, singing, or his gun is singing, into the window of the van.

43

Doctor Murray, as has already been mentioned, was short and fat. And underneath him, he had even shorter legs. Well, the antics of him, if ever he got excited, you wouldn't see in a circus. The way he started conducting himself on the lawn was, they said afterwards, priceless. All he had to do was tell the good woman to get inside the door. But the sound of the gunfire must have left him speechless, for he started flapping about her and manhandling her by the back of the neck towards the porch, and of course, she must have thought he was about to ravish her, for she started resisting him. And the pair of them on the lawn was, as they say, a play.

Afterwards the doctor did go over to see if he could, as a doctor, do anything for the breadman. But there wasn't much anyone could do for the breadman then, without a mop and a bucket of water.

'Doctor,' said Sarah later on, 'there's this old woman in a green coat with a red scarf, Mrs Keane I think is her name, and she's always watching me. One day she threw rosary beads into my face. Honest. And she's always telling people stories about me after Mass.'

Through separate pairs of spectacles Doctor Murray and Sarah scrutinised each other.

'I'm going to have to do something about it, doctor.'

But the doctor was less and less help.

The world, Jesus said to her, *is not a mistake. There is a reason for everything.*

The image of the broken face in the van remained with Sarah for a long time. It would come and sit on the sofa beside her when she was watching the television, so that she couldn't continue. It made her dark towards the village and one evening, while she was watching *Coronation Street,* Marian phoned to say that Mrs Keane had taken a stroke and all Sarah felt like saying was, good, I'm glad.

Everybody, the entire village, was shocked and dismayed by the killing of the breadman. But nobody had the foggiest clue as to how or why he had been shot. As Sarah's husband often said, it's not for people to be too political. No. Lave that to the political boys.

44

Sarah was amazed by the increasing beauty of the cherry tree in the doctor's garden.

'Sarah,' the doctor said, 'you're a good housewife and you're just going through a bit of a rough patch.'

Marian begged her not to listen to him. Why couldn't they both go away to London for a fortnight? Having a shopping holiday? But Sarah wouldn't listen to that. All Sarah wanted to do was sit in the doctor's garden and look at the cherry tree, and talk to Jesus. (Not that she mentioned the latter to Marian.)

So there you have it. Doctor Murray was phoning James Gullion daily and telling him he should be more strict with her. James Gullion was phoning God-knows-who at all hours of the night. Marian was gone off on a tangent, reading books on female psychology. And Sarah, in a blue cardigan they had bought her when she came out of hospital, was sitting under the doctor's cherry tree, watching the compassionate face of Christ whispering her name, gazing at her through the branches.

Mrs Gullion had gone into a dark little corner of her own house, brooding over many things unmentionable.

After the shooting the streets were more than usually deserted. Loneliness clung even tighter to everyone. They would stay in bed for hours. Forgetting it. A communal remorse.

Sarah was in a long dream about Australia, watching the doctor's tree go from strength to strength in the unexpected early summer. At night she could sleep alone. Sometimes. And other times she couldn't. He was strict about this. And then there were nights he never came home at all. Then she could hear Christ, at the back of the house, barefoot, walking through the grass.

There were times she couldn't stop herself eating. Rice crispies, rice crispies, rice crispies; there was nothing she wouldn't do for rice crispies.

She would spend hours at the dressing table when he was not in the house, arranging the little bottles. On the night he would insist on her, she imagined herself as a slave, chained to the bed. He thought things were going to be all right then. But she was not imagining herself as his slave; she would close her eyes and think of someone else.

And after such nights, she too was inclined to lie under the covers until the middle of the day. OK, she would say to Marian, OK, I'm sorry, though the room was empty.

She would dream then of a redbricked suburban house in Australia which was her own. And in it there was a long room, all for herself. It had high ceilings, and French windows at the far end which opened out on golden lawns. And in this house she had many male servants – European and Oriental – who obeyed her every command. Nimble dark-skinned Filipinos and blond muscular Germans standing at every corner; some clothed in white uniforms, some naked and some in delicate frills. They dusted the furniture in her room and ran the bath. They brought her trays of fruit – fig and guava – and pitchers of iced tea. Some of them – ooh, this she thought was delicious – some of them wore, as well as she could imagine it, chastity belts – golden girdles that prevented erection, to be opened at her discretion by the keys she held round her neck. In her dream she called them her creatures or toys and they, needless to say, adored her. When her bath was ready, in the vast marble bathing chamber, she would walk like an empress to it while her toys lined the corridors and bowed.

But no matter how she tried to contain the images, they always expanded like smoke and then disintegrated. Her suburban house was, within minutes, a huge mansion and then a castle. But when she opened her eyes, she found that the clouds had covered the sun and the room was dark and dusty, and even her lace knickers were a shabby tribute to the elegance that ached in her imagination. So she was forced to wash. To clean herself in that bathroom which was so rank with his peculiar smells, his dribbled toothpaste and his shaving cream. The tang of aftershave. His facial hair speckling the sink, and his old socks on the floor beside the toilet bowl.

James Gullion was more than strict. He was suspicious. Going out in the morning he often forgot his keys and then when he returned, perhaps halfway through the morning, he would bang impatiently on the kitchen window. Marian claimed this was a trick to keep Sarah housebound because she was afraid to go out for a minute once she saw his keys on the hall table.

What frightened her most of all was sarcasm, and it was hardening her against him. One evening, for example, he noticed a glossy magazine on top of the television set. He picked it up and flicked through the images of women in pink satin and girls pouting the textures of myriad lipsticks and cosmetics, and he crossed his legs and ridiculed it for over half an hour. She stared at the television and pretended not to notice, but inside she was thinking of his body stripped and manacled and trussed from the rafter in the garage like a side of beef. She ought to stick a sanitary towel in his gob; that would shut him up.

Marian said she was bloody right. You're bloody right, Sarah, she would say, bloody right.

Sarah thought she would be better being loved by someone. Anyone. Even Marian, if she had the interest. The doctor just told her to take more exercise and Sarah went on eating packet after packet of rice crispies.

Sometimes she was jealous of Marian. Especially on Friday nights in the hotel, when Marian was at the bar collecting drinks and chatting with Doctor Murray, and Sarah thought she looked so capable.

Sometimes there was country-and-western music and a bar extension till two in the morning. While the men drank, the girls waltzed, jived or quickstepped round in couples. It was only when Sarah said, 'Will you dance with me, Marian?' that she realised how hard Marian was. Marian, she began to realise, would never dance with her.

All day long eating rice crispies, listening to the radio. Friday nights watching schoolgirls is no way to live.

But who's going to dance with me if Marian doesn't? she asked Jesus.

But Jesus never replied.

You should always make sure you're dancing with someone, she said, *even if it's only a dream.*

When you shoot someone, she said in a dream, *you're only shooting yourself.*

But still Jesus wouldn't answer.

Her eyes were downcast following the tiles on the corridor. There were black and white tiles on the floor and green ones on the walls. They didn't match. There was a man in a dressing gown watching her. A young girl in a green nylon housecoat flung her bucket of Savlon on the floor, frightening Sarah. The young girl's movements were brusque; her heels clicking on the tiles.

Sarah passed her and screamed, 'Fuck you, fuck you. I want a bag of. . . apples. And an umbrella. It's been raining all day.'

Little heed was paid to this tantrum. But it was critical. Sarah even took off her glasses and flung them on the floor where they exploded into smithereens. That too was significant. Sarah was attempting a comeback. Something in her was going to fight. The door between us is going to be opened, she said to herself. A little more blather. A little more screaming at the white-capped nurses; fuck you, fucker.

So many beds were wheeled up and down the corridors that it often reminded Sarah of a main street. Then she looked around and wondered who was causing the fuss and finally, in a moment of clarity, she realised it was herself.

Later that night the nurse with the kind white shoes asked her why she had been screaming for apples. Sarah said it was because she wanted apples. She wanted to eat, she said. Eat healthy food. And if her husband came, she could offer him one. It would look good. The nurse was kind but strong.

'Your husband never visits you, Sarah.'

'Well that's not my fault. Anyway, it's always raining,' Sarah retorted. 'Why can't I have an umbrella and go for walks? Everyone else has something to do. You're the nurses. The other girls go round cleaning everything. That fella there keeps watching me and shouting at people. I need something as well. It's not fair.'

'It's not fair,' she said to Marian. But Marian told her to stop whinging.

Still, the nurse with the soft white shoes thought there was a lot of sense to it.

Sarah wasn't going to remain the same for ever. Her personality wasn't static. Always in process, it was bound to change this way and that, depending on the circumstances, pressures and dangers of the experiences she was living through.

Nor was she a saint. In fact as a young girl she had a room of her own for a few years and she often stayed in it, alone, until it became rank with poisonous shadows. Then she would suck them in and be possessed by them before going out to flail around at the world with a knife. And it's strange how a woman possessed in such a way can be described, even in the modern world, as a little witch.

These were merely passing moods in her childhood. The time of the month, a teacher might say. Speaking of which, Sarah had always felt since 'that thing' began that she had given in to the way the world wanted her to be. She was vanquished by it in a manner she could not comprehend. But it tortured her. Month after month. And had she not given in again to the way the world wanted her to be when she became a wife? For goodness' sake, she was only twenty-two at the time. A child. And how old was she now? Thirty? Thirty-two?

'Jesus Christ, Marian,' she said, 'where has my life gone?' Her life must be going on somewhere else.

The spectacles were her first victory. She insisted on the new pair being fashionable. And they were. Well they weren't really; they were steel-rimmed and in style, a slight variation on the broken pair. But her assertiveness about them when she came out of hospital, buying them in Dublin and so forth, was crucial. She had taken the first chip of plaster off the wall.

And there was more than James Gullion who remarked on the

50

difference. All about there, men knew a sullen woman when they saw one. And that wan, they began saying, is getting right cross in herself. Men who masturbate into their vests are essentially cowards. Though the woman who is the keeper of the knife in a conversation is their most precious terror. Half the time James Gullion slept alone, and Sarah washed his vests. But she was to change all that. She took possession again of the matrimonial suite. She would lie on the bed waiting for him to come home. It unnerved him to find her still awake, reading her glossy magazines. She must be after something, he thought. But she wasn't. Just when he was beginning to thaw out, she would close the magazine, flick off her light switch and fall asleep.

When she dozed in the armchair in the drawing room, the room became full of shadows. It was as if she were knitting something invisible. When he entered, she would smile (he would have called it a crazy smile) and ask, what do you want?

He told her it wasn't her room.

'It's more a cell than a room,' she replied, 'but I've always had my own room anyway, no thanks to you.'

He really hadn't a clue what she was talking about but he didn't like the sound of it.

Every dark moment in the past returned and strengthened her. She could cut him backwards and forwards. It was like suddenly discovering she could drive. She never knew she could do that.

You'll not get me into a lunatic asylum again, she'd snap – you'll not get me to wipe your arse for you – you better phone your mother – when he became helpless about sorting out his underwear for the wash.

And at night, when through drink he had got his way with her, she would take revenge by staring at him and smiling, as if she had been observing something faintly ridiculous. Some nights she was in the spare room. Some nights, in the double bed. It was driving him crazy. Some nights he hated sleeping with her. Hated the smell of her. And sure enough, as if she knew, that was the night she'd be there waiting for him. Driving home from an agricultural meeting, his heart pumping. Going into his room and finding that she was there waiting for him. And afterwards, switching on the light and asking something irrelevant, like did you ring your mother about the roof?

They were so cold and untender to each other during daylight that her intimacy at night was frightening and it disgusted him. And the very night after a political meeting or a few pints with the lads that he came down the hall to the spare room and fumbled on the door with his fingers in a pathetic attempt at tenderness, his cock raring to be at it, he would, needless to say, find she had locked the door (locked the door!) so that an argument would develop. And she'd be in there laughing at him and telling him to feck off with himself. By jingo, those were nights he swore to himself that he'd destroy her. I'm telling ye, he'd say to himself, I'll destroy her.

But she had him beat. James Gullion's erect penis was a matter to be taken seriously. A mysterious and sacred thing. To laugh at it? Goodness, it was incomprehensible! Yet there she was, behind the door, laughing at it. The most noble thing in the world, when a man becomes a lion, and approaches his beloved. And she laughs. It was blasphemy. A laughter that persisted through the winter; that hung around the house all day; that twinkled in her eyes as she stared out of the shadows at him; and that was gradually having a withering effect on the majesty of James Gullion.

Marian was nothing less than delighted. She found Sarah handsome beyond comparison when she talked that way and she never tired of teasing out every detail of their sexual warfare. Though there were times too after a long conversation with Marian when Sarah felt like an empty rag that had been squeezed of its juice.

Did James begin to hear the echo of laughter when Marian looked at him? When any woman smiled at him? James was in deep trouble. Two fields from the bungalow there was a cluster of trees, an old burial ground for stillborn and unbaptised babies. Even with the trees as shelter, it was a windy, lonesome hilltop and the wind made the trees cry out. On the pretence of looking at the cattle, James would go up there and curse her for hours. She was either a witch or a lunatic. James was still a young man, hardly forty. He was healthy. But he was afraid of her. Yes. There was no doubt about it. The world was turning upside down. And no amount of drink or stories, or the magazines that get passed about, or generally sniffing around, could get it the right way up again.

The hostilities would continue, intensify, and suddenly cease. There was no explaining it. Some night he is sleeping alone, jaded, no longer able to do battle with her. The house is silent. They are both awake. In separate rooms. The silence intensifies. Neither can sleep. She knocks on his door. She is wearing a pair of his pyjamas. She enters, sits on the bed, strokes his forehead. He is not afraid of her now. He is a child. With just a shaft of light from the hall they watch each other. They have no sophisticated language for this moment. They must move by instinct. Every move of an eye is a huge risk. Until eventually, and without preliminary discussion, she closes the bedroom door and slips into the space he makes for her. And before you know it, James Gullion's world is the right way up again.

The next morning she packs his lunch as usual. Two cheese sandwiches in a blue plastic box. She maintains her usual silence during breakfast. So does he. But when he stops later in the day, he finds alongside the cheese sandwiches a large quarter of apple tart. Such is life.

And behold, it came to pass,
She was with child.

Doctor Murray made the authoritative examination. Sarah could hear the *One O'clock News* in the next room as he addressed her in his surgery. After much fussing about with bottles of urine and reports from laboratories, he announced to her from behind his desk that she was pregnant.

'You're pregnant,' he declared. He reminded her of Humpty Dumpty.

'Yes,' she said, 'I know.'

He stared at her then through his jamjar-bottom spectacles, and thought – dear me, she is a droll hen.

Do you think that the troubles in the early years of a marriage are over just because you get pregnant? Of course not. In the months that followed, her husband grew irritated by her washing and dressing, which he told her seemed to be unending. Admittedly there was, in general, less tension between them as he sat eating his porridge and eggs in the morning and she stood at the sink by the window in her dressing gown and slippers, sipping gallons of sweet milk. There were some reasons why he was glad about her pregnancy. He had the bedroom to himself, with no fear of her annoying him or his wrinkled penis that seemed to have forgotten its highest office most of the time.

Gosh, she thought one day, I've banished Marian. (This was not true, but the sight of Sarah's stomach reminded Marian of much that was painful and she had, consequently, stayed away.)

Dear Jesus, today I lit the fire for you. Why don't you come and we could listen to the gramophone or the BBC? In the after-noons when he is out working. I've grown tired of my creatures. I cut their heads off so often and spanked their tails so raw that there is only a flitter of them left.

She could imagine him standing behind her as she whispered it. She could almost imagine him stroking her hair.

I feel like a well today. What will come out of me?

She put his photograph up on the wall of the spare room for protection. At night she kissed it.

You know how much I love you.

She could imagine him pecking her on the cheek and she would say good night and fall immediately asleep. Until morning.

The truth will come out of me today.

She thought, could Marian possibly be jealous?

'There's something up,' her husband said to Doctor Murray. Which was not an appropriate phrase since he had come to the good doctor to enquire whether there was anything in the world that might be found for his ailing virility.

The doctor was confused.

'There's definitely something up,' he repeated, 'with the wife.'

'How exactly do you mean?' the doctor asked. (Does he not know she is pregnant? the doctor mused.)

'I mean, doctor, that she's making very free. She has a smile on her face like a Cheshire cat. There's something up and I'm kinna unaisy that she might be making a bit free.'

What might James Gullion have felt if he discovered that the root of his jealousy was a holy picture on the wall? There's no point trying to follow the tangle of confusion that ensued for half an hour in the doctor's surgery – or rather in the doctor's imagination: connect the known pregnancy of the wife with the alleged impotency of the husband, and the husband's unease that the wife was making a bit free – Doctor Murray began to feel he was getting entwined in a soap opera.

Sarah's pregnancy was a journey into the deepest caverns of her self. Her past, her college days, and the city faded. They were remote and unreal. She was becoming aware of her self at last. She was on course for the interior. It was a vocation; she was being called away, not just from the past but from the trouble-some life of Casnagee. Called in to be mother of a new life. The compassionate face of Christ always travelling with her.

Her husband became intensely suspicious. The village more deeply convinced of her lunacy. All about the bungalow, the roads meandered round hills, to and from other bungalows. And he was away all day. Far away. Who knows, he thought, what gentlemen are calling?

Sometimes when a toilet fails to flush, people leave a saucepan of water by the bowl. In a remote rural toilet the saucepan might be there for weeks. (All to do with the water pressure.)

He didn't know what was going on in his own house. That's what he thought. And sometimes he wished that he could take her by the hair and fling her headfirst against the wall. By jingo, he thought. If only he could get away with it.

How did he know the baby was his? All the riding they did in ten years hadn't produced one. Why now? She had done it to spite him. To defy him. To estrange him. To leave him outside.

Saucepans of water in the toilet. What were they for but only to annoy him? And then she insisted on calling a plumber. Insisted, if ye don't mind. But what did she want bringing plumbers into the house for? Eh? The young McCarthy lad, with his copper pipes and screwdrivers. All day in his house. Fiddling with something as private as the toilet. And her in the condition she was in? Not right. Not bloody right. If there was going to be a plumber, then he could come on a day when he could be watched.

And finally, the ultimate irritation, one morning when he was sitting on the bowl and discovered that she had taken the saucepan away. Why the bloody hell does she do that, he thought, but only to annoy me?

Sarah.

Sa-rah.

S-a-ra-h, wheredidyouleavethebloodysaucepan?

No reply.

You see, there was no point in explaining to him that she had removed it because he had been complaining about it under his feet, day in, day out, for a week. No. No point at all. For she was far away from him. So far, in fact, that she was only vaguely aware of his rasping voice at all.

And she had her own preoccupations. And pains. Pains inside herself, and it scared her, and she was afraid they would come for her and put her in the hospital again; not the maternity hospital but the other place, and dispossess her of her baby. With their technology.

One day she would get a craving for it to be a boy. The next day she would be craving for mint sweets and couldn't care less about the sex. At night she would debate with the face of Christ about how to approach the business. Should she phone Marian and make sure she was around in the later weeks? Should she reach out to her husband or Doctor Murray? Worse still, would she panic and lean on them out of fear?

The holy picture on the wall was a consolation. Its power not to be underestimated. Sarah's belly got larger and she was like a plum, getting juicier and juicier.

A strange aroma filled the bungalow, which got up her husband's nose. Sometimes he found things in the kitchen sink that he could make neither head nor tail of.

For her part Sarah took no notice of anything. She fed chickens. She cooked chickens. She sat in the drawing room staring at the carpet's blue pile. It was all the same to her. The names of things began to slip away from the things themselves. So she called the door a gate one morning when he was going out.

'Close the gate,' she said, 'it's cold.' She meant the front door.

The saucepans became pots. The teapot, a jug. And for other things she invented new names: the hibby jibby, the tong tong, and the shooter. And she would waddle round the house alone talking a sort of private language to herself; duckety duckety duck.

She was not aware how deeply troubled her husband was over this solitude. Though she hardly ever left the house now, he was mad raving jealous and it was building inside him like steam in a pressure cooker. That he could find no likely rascal tormented him all the more. And her presence in the house was always like two people laughing at him. He wasn't being paid the attention he deserved. The attention he was entitled to from a wife.

She was bright and lively in herself.

Dear Jesus who knows how beautiful this child will be. Who knows all the things he will wear and all the places he will visit.

Dear Jesus, I would be entwined with you for ever. To feel you on every inch of me.

And there were times when she would have enticed Jesus off his cross and invited him into intimacies not common in Catholic devotions; intimacies with her neck, tummy, breast and bum. Mornings when the compassionate face of Christ slipped off the wall to become her Lord and Master in a tenderness not known to the Pope.

Sarah was flip-flopping to the kitchen in her slippers and dressing gown when he roared.

'Sa-rah.'

She wasn't aware of him.

'I'll not have anybody interfering in my house. You understand?'

But she was flip-flopping to the kitchen. To make the porridge. Hardly aware of him thundering beside her until he smacked her across the back of the head with his fist and bounced her forehead off the top of the cooker.

He was lucky it was so early in the day. Had it happened after the pubs closed, and with the way he used to shoot off his mouth about her, they might have suspected him. But eight o'clock in the morning is not a time normally associated with beating the wife. Men are expected to have more on their minds at that hour of the day.

It wasn't so much the bang on the head as the way she fell on the floor that did the damage.

'Ah Jimmy, go up and get the doctor,' she screamed.

He did.

She heard the car roaring down the lane. Then she lay there, knowing that the child was choking or suffocating or drowning – she didn't know which – but she knew all the same that it was going away. She could feel it inside her, crying out at her, and she wanted at least to let it know that it was not her, no, it was not her fault.

She looked up at the Sacred Heart picture on the wall. She could tell the very second when it died. She looked up from the floor at the picture on the wall and shouted, *Jesus. Fuck you.*

When the man in the post office heard the story two hours later from the creamery man, who heard it from the husband when he was collecting the milk, the post-office man threw his eyes up to heaven and whistled.

'Well what sort of an eejit is she anyhow?' he asked.

It was the firm conviction of the community that such a tragedy was only to be expected, taking into account that the girl was not the full shilling from the start.

Sarah was put to sleep when she was in the ambulance and when she woke that afternoon in a private room in the hospital, there was a nurse sitting beside her bed, holding her hand. She was a lovely little girl of a nurse, Sarah thought.

'You lost the baby,' she said.

Sarah wanted to ask how it died. Or where was the foetus? Or would it be buried or burned or what? But she didn't She was near strangled in herself by the shame of it all. She did not blame herself for losing the child. But she blamed herself for not being careful enough. She had been careless. Unaware of dangers. Half asleep.

That evening Marian came with chocolates. A beautiful box of milk chocolates.

In those villages the story of one woman was, as likely as not, the story of every other woman. And yet the funny thing was that the similarity of every story with the next lent not credibility but doubt to each one.

If a woman was foolish enough to reveal her troubles to someone in the basket-weaving class, the tendency was to reject it with the attitude – ah sure we heard that before. By listening once, who was to say an entire can of worms would not open? Certain things were too terrible to believe. And who, then, could a woman turn to when her husband had turned cold if not the compassionate face of Christ, to be comforted, gazed upon and slayed?

So on and on it went in the kitchens of a hundred bungalows. The long cleanup that never ended. The hoovering of dining rooms. Under the chair legs. Popping in and out to each other like yoyos at eleven o'clock for coffee. But not the truth. So isolated and alone that they could be trusted, even among each other, to avoid any terrible truths. Avoid anything deeper than what was the last thing discussed on the morning chat show on the radio. Like the size of the Irish potato. Now there was a subject to get dug into.

It all added up to a lot of women with dead faces staring into each other, saying less than nothing. See ya after lunch – whatever that meant. But they were always getting together again – after lunch or after tea or tomorrow or some time in the rosy future when they would find a way to say it all. A time that never arrived.

And how well, in the meantime, did they learn to make beds? To fold men's pyjamas. To gather fluff off the couch. To puff a blue cushion, with one little pat, into newness again. And the curtains? Well, the mind simply boggles at the frills that hung in such beautiful pastels from kitchen window, and everywhere else. The furry cover for the toilet seat? Nay! The furry cover on the toilet seat that matched the curtains on the toilet window. The furry cover on the toilet seat that matched the pink plastic of the laundry bin.

Every room tingling with delicate feminine fragrances, squirted from aerosols stored in the press beneath the kitchen sink. Mardyke the Magician. Take a pair of underwear. With skid marks. Wash them. Twiddle dee dum, twiddle dee dee, and they smell like roses. (That's from the aerosol you squirt a bit when you're ironing.)

Drinking stale coffee and staring at the ridiculous washing machine in the kitchen; the antichrist which took in that which was dirty and in its baptism made it whiter than white.

In the meantime, those women grew dumpy and began to smell of detergent. But what does that matter? They became neglectful of their clothes as they pottered round the house. But again, what does that matter? Effectively they had become invisible. The house was pretty. Yes. And in the evenings the men came into their houses.

After Sarah lost the child, she could no longer look her husband in the eye. At all times in his presence she kept her head bowed. She resisted her fantasies, thinking them to have been unlucky and, in that sense, not unconnected to the child's death.

She would make his dinner. Bacon and cabbage. She would stand over the sink with her back to him, as he ate and listened to the radio news. Then she would dish out for herself the cold cabbage from the saucepan, and the bacon he had not eaten, and she would punish herself with this food, for as is the case with many people, even the smell of it disgusted her. But she ate it.

There were other foods turned her stomach after the miscarriage. Chickens, for example. But she cooked them. She cleaned them and cooked them and ate them.

Her dreams were unlucky. Instead of dreaming she needed

61

to give in to her husband. He was her only salvation. It was in resisting him that all had gone wrong. She was over thirty; it was time she came to terms with it. She was a married woman. It was to him, at last, that she must open her heart. Confess her self. Pride would get her nowhere. There was no escaping that.

One evening she sat down beside him at the table and looked at him. She said she wanted to talk. She said it was all her fault and she realised that now. She trembled as she spoke, for she knew there was a gate opening that she would not afterwards be able to close. She had been a bad wife. But she had been sick. Now she needed help. His help. So she prostrated herself before him and was exhilerated. She would have nothing more to do with Christ, she thought. And she would not pray again.

Her husband listened, as one who is wise; who is impressed neither with denial nor confession but who will, rather, weigh up the evidence. That is to say he took flashing glances at her as he continued unhindered through his rasher, his two sausages and his pot of strong tea.

Now don't take your eyes off the story for a moment. You mustn't miss anything. Yes, Sarah's unquiet spirit was as safe as a trout in a frozen pond. She'd be going nowhere for a long time to come. Maybe nothing much else was likely to happen. But who knows?

The compassionate face of Christ had grown longer whiskers and twisted itself in her mind into the terrible smiling face of a cat. All she could see of him were the accusing eyes that followed her round the house, smiled at her from the icons that hung on neighbours' walls or behind the altar in the chapel. Some music in her had finally been turned off. Finally? It certainly appeared so.

Her meal times she spent with her husband. For the rest of the day or night she laughed at the silliest of things. She whitewashed the walls of the byre and the outhouses. She told herself it was an act of love. She had wounded him, and every brush stroke was a scooping out of the wounds she had done to him. When he looked at her, she opened everything to him, asserting over and over again her guilt and shame. And he was not unimpressed.

But who did she blame besides herself? Old Cat's Eyes. Some dark journey he had led her! Yes sir, she said. Cat's Eyes.

One day she spilled the cornflakes right onto the table. Did that stir even the mildest storm between the happy couple? Certainly not. She roared laughing and turned to him in a sweep of apologies.

'Goodness,' she said, 'I'm all butterfingers.'

'Will you be all right on your own?' he asked.

'Yes, yes, of course, it's just, y'know, that time of the month.'

Of course.

She was not unlike the women around her. Like fish in a closed world when the oxygen runs scarce. They look up through the ice and blame the cat's paw for their situation. All intensely lonely. Longing for something without quite knowing what it might be. Their entire lives spent swimming about in the breathless air of their husbands' world; a political ambiance as lively as stale water, without knowing anything else, without dreaming of the fish that could fly or considering the delicious taste of being caught by the cat's paw, and released.

The cat's eyes they worshipped because they intuitively feared them.

She was not interested in her husband's business. The arguments of ancestors that whispered behind the trees. The long hours her husband spent 'away' at nights. Or the long hours with other men in the kitchen, drinking whiskey, fingering their own wounds.

No, she was not unlike the women around her. And yes, it took years. She was losing her accent and her memory. She swam with them now. Mumbled a few prayers with them at the back of the chapel.

She learned to drive. She drove from village to village. Bungalows dotting the rolling, verdant landscape to the right. Whitewashed grocery stores in the middle of nowhere. Tractors and lorries. Women with prams. The river on her left. And as she drove she listened to the local pirate radio station, blanketing the vision with country-and-western music. Every day she did this until she passed the test. The driving licence became her new identity card.

But could she not be rescued by the local women's group? No. In the jungle of windows there was a different agenda. There were political priorities. There was no escape. Even Marian began to sound out of place as Sarah found other women. Real women. Sensible women. And they would knock on her door and ask well, how's the boss? And she would say, ah, sure he's fine. Women here were girls, and the girls were virgins laced into tightly held postures in the hotel lounge, where only the hysterical giggles betrayed their muffled desire.

Her landscape was a tight little basket of fruit, field, stone, beef, and cat's eyes. The world was two sides of a river. A necklace of graveyards where warriors were buried. A river in which someone would occasionally drown themselves. A place where certain unmentionable and often distasteful things just had to be done. And where a woman had no place to interfere. Keep two pairs of everything in the hot-press and ask no questions, as Sarah said.

Sarah had little to either forget or remember. She had had barely reason to believe in herself until her husband came along.

As has been said, she was dim. Extremely ordinary. In her childhood and adolescence she was merely an eyewitness to history. To other girls' stories. They who were suffering. Those who were battered. By gosh, she thought, would they have laughed if she had mentioned her little red statue of Jesus she kept beside the bed to talk with? Her little man she wondered at? When her sisters were suffering the most unmentionable atrocities.

Those horrid rich teachers who slept in huge houses and talked of Paris, Chagall and sex. Fuck them. That was her word for them. And, kiss me, Jesus, she would say, opening the prayer book, kiss me with your words.

She was deprived of punishment. She had no welts on her hands to show off. And she craved, if not welts and blisters then certainly her little bit of the story.

Watching other girls caned. The shock and sordid pleasure. There was something very desirable about being caned by refined, educated people. People who had been to the opera house in Paris. But she was never taken up to anyone's room for the slaps. Or the chocolates all the girls got afterwards from Miss McEntee.

And then years later, in college, meeting all Marian's friends with all the same stories; but this time adult versions – spanked not by nuns or mad brittle spinsters but battered and scarred by husbands, boyfriends, pimps, brutes of every shape and size. Perhaps, she thought, I haven't lived until I suffer. It was fair to say that when she met her husband, she began to suffer. And now, after a long resistance, she had come to accept that this was life.

Had she imparted these ideas to Marian, she would have got a quick retort. But under the new dispensation of Sarah's submission to her husband, Marian feared the worst and stayed away. Sarah had no inclination to phone her either. The bungalow was her cloister. Marian, Christ or any other intruding presence was banished. She had but one Lord and Master now and it was for him she lived.

All this submission was not achieved without the greatest efforts. And she was afraid. She woke at three in the morning in a state of heat and tension, her body dripping sweat. Her husband's face issuing bad breath, like a volcano, into the darkness beside her. She went to the kitchen, sat there, her bare feet on the cold tiles, gulping glasses of water. The following morning she wouldn't even remember the event.

She lived in a bungalow on the edge of a village. She lived there. She could travel the hall at night in her sleep. What was wrong with that?

Besides her sleepwalking there were other signs. Somebody sent her a kitchen wall clock. Battery run. Big red yoke. Came in the post. Well, the only nail on the kitchen wall was holding up the Sacred Heart. So out he went.

And her kidneys didn't improve after the miscarriage. She could spend ages sitting on the toilet seat in pain trying to pee.

But she could accept everything with the philosophy: this is what it is to be me. To have a life. Was anything ever going to explode again? She wrote in her diary:

> I am reading the papers again. And watching television. I am not angry any more. The politics is very interesting when you can understand it.

How pathetic. No one gave the remotest shit what she thought about politics.

'I am getting control,' she wrote at last. 'I am coming out of it.'

She was. She could now talk to the vet or submit to her husband's desires without the slightest emotion. Doctor Murray could potter around for half an hour without her being in the slightest bit embarrassed. After all, he was a doctor.

The only time she released emotion was watching the television. Reading the newspapers. Or listening to the radio. That made her blood boil. Politics. Politics. Politics. The real world, as James called it. Better have an interest in politics than go mad. She wrote in her diary one day:

> I need to say something to myself. I need to remind myself of something. But I'm afraid even as I write that I will destroy it, or forget it.

After that she abandoned her diary for ever.

The long war.
The killers who know the victims,
and the victims' widows
who know the killers.

That dark oppressive intimacy
every time you rub shoulders
with a neighbour and behave with civility.

The war that must go on because it is one's duty
to those who have already given their lives.

To those who are already dead.

As the old storytellers used to say when they were on the verge of a major twist in the tale, things rested so for years. Things rested so for years, and then. And then things change. No one can completely desert themselves.

Sarah's routines had remained unchanged for a very long time. Until the day she met Lord Coco. She was walking down Grafton Street on one of those bright fresh mornings in springtime when she would take the bus to Dublin for a bit of nostalgia, as she liked to call it.

If anyone from her college days had chanced to bump into her on the street they would have found her reasonably well preserved for a woman now in her late thirties. Slightly plump, perhaps. A glazed look in her eyes, as if she were thinking of something else, but still the same old dim docile Sarah. Sometimes too, when she was listening to someone, she would take a slow deep inward breath and let it out again. Sometimes she would find her eyes watering at the most sentimental of country-and-western songs or at the silliest of soap operas on the television. But only close friends might notice those things and she had sustained few friendships from her college days. Anyway, on this particular morning she met no one. That is, except Lord Coco. Coco was a man in his late fifties, with grey hair and a moustache like the twin tails of a bird. He wore a bowler hat and a long striped shirt which went down below his knees, and he danced in his black shoes to the accompaniment of music from a tape recorder on the pavement beside him.

There must have been forty people standing about on the street enjoying him. Such entertainers usually made Sarah tense, as if the lawlessness of their frolics were a threat to her.

But on this occasion she overcame her rational self and paused for a moment on the fringe of the crowd. It was, after all, such a delightful day.

Almost immediately, his enormous brown eyes met hers and he winked. This innocent salutation frightened the daylights out of her. She deferred her eyes to the pavement, raised a thumb and forefinger to her left ear and passed briskly down the street.

She purchased a mug of coffee in Bewley's. She settled herself at an empty table, lit a cigarette and discovered, before she had inhaled twice or even touched her coffee, that Coco had sailed into the restaurant, perched himself as nifty as a bird on the seat across the table from her and was staring straight into her thick spectacles. He winked. She nearly choked on the smoke.

'They're bad for you,' he said.

Sarah and Lord Coco left the restaurant about half an hour later, together. If anyone then, from her salad days, had crossed her path, they would have remarked on more than the fact that she was walking alongside a most eccentric human being. They would have noted, even in those small bespectacled eyes, a certain hint of fire.

She went home that evening as usual on the evening bus. She cooked her husband's dinner, enquired about the health of his mother, watched the television and went to bed. This obedient wife had by now developed an Ulster accent, she was a punctual member of the basket-making class on Wednesday nights, and a member of the Altar Society which kept the chapel fresh with flowers. She had mended herself well, they said. But the community was off guard. Sarah had merely held her breath for a long time. And then suddenly the cat's paw had crashed through the surface of the pool, on a spring day on Grafton Street.

It was almost six o'clock on the last day of May. Sarah was waiting in the back yard. The kitchen door was open and she could hear the Ulster news on the BBC. The cat was licking itself on the kitchen windowsill. The apple trees on the hill beyond the yard were coming into full flower. In the distance she could hear the sound of tractors; the first cuts of soilage. Her husband would not be home till after dark. The main headline on the news was that another UDR man had been blown up somewhere, but Sarah no longer cared. She reached her hand out instinctively and stroked the cat's head. It purred. She went close to it so that their noses touched.

Then a white Bedford van turned into the yard and stopped abruptly. For that second she wanted to turn back. It was a beautiful bungalow. The yard was a dazzle of whitewashed sheds. The fields and lakes about her were reassuring. The cat would always be there, looking in the window at her. Always needing attention. Her husband would always come home. Well, even a prison is difficult to leave after so long but she knew that the chance would never come again.

She had consulted no one. She had simply posted letters. And one special one to James Gullion. After that moment in the post office when she let the envelopes fall from her fingers into the mouth of the postbox, she knew there was no turning back.

Lord Coco had his name painted in gay circus colours on both sides of the van. In smaller letters underneath was written:

CLOWN AND MAGICIAN
International Reputation

He stepped up to her in the same white shirt with blue fish-bone

72

stripes, the same bowler hat, and the same wonderful moustache. He looked about the yard nervously and enquired, 'You haven't changed your mind, have you?'

Of course she hadn't. It was just that she was taking nothing with her except a shoulder bag with some of her most personal belongings. There was a good reason for that. She wanted to make sure that James would not be suspicious. He would think she had gone up to the mother's house for the night. It would be twenty-four hours before he knew what was going on or be able to follow her.

So she locked the door. What a moment. Sixteen years. Now she was locking the door and dropping the key down the drain. She hopped into the passenger seat and the van pulled away. Down the long lane. Her eyes blinking at the lake in the distance, the trim green fields, and the long street of the village. Her husband's house in the distance, on a green hill, smaller and smaller till it was only a dot.

Mind you, the visitation of his lordship to those villages would not have gone unnoticed. As he told her, he alighted more than twice, at petrol pumps and sweet shops, looking for directions. In one place, which was full of children with school bags on their way home, he had even produced a box of coloured feathers and offered them to the shopkeeper for a price.

'They go down very well with the younger ones,' he asserted, but the pursed lips of the man in the brown shop coat were disdainful.

In the weeks that followed, they were to say of Sarah that she had been taken off by the devil himself.

When Lord Coco's van had travelled far enough to have shaken the dust of those villages from its tyres, Sarah no longer gave a single thought to the past. There were mountains and oceans ahead of them. The white van would go up many's a high hill and down many's a low valley. Coco kept his eye on the road and was, for the most part, silent. Sarah lifted a large brown envelope from the floor, took from it the frayed manuscript entitled 'The Prophesies of Lord Coco', and began to read.

Hear ye now, all ye my daughters, for the time cometh.
Hear ye now, ye that dwell in the land of Fermanagh,
and in the land of Down,
and in the far-flung glens of Antrim,
and in the reaches of Omagh and Londonderry,
which is also called Derry.
Listen unto me for the sword is already in my hand.
Listen unto me, ye daughters that weep by the Bann, the Lagan,
the Foyle and the Erne.
A time of wrath is at hand.
And a time of deliverance.
Hear me, ye that hath plenty for the mouth,
for now thy humiliation is at hand.
Thou shalt behold it, and it shall be before your eyes.
And ye shall be brought unto it, and be vanquished thereby.
Hear me now, ye that are listening.

'You're mad,' she said, putting down the manuscript.
The van was whizzing through Cavan.
'I make it up as I go along,' he said, 'but it's great for drawing a crowd.'

And they whizzed further than Cavan. In fact there was nowhere that the white van did not go; the rear full of blankets and sleeping bags, the back windows plastered with stickers from the 1960s urging the world to make love and not war, for war is ugly and love is lovely.

Like his more illustrious namesake, Coco too was a clown. He was six foot, must have weighed over fifteen stone and, when fully undressed, revealed a portly aspect. So much fat, in fact, that he could not see his sword. Yes *sword*, for he called it that himself and then roared laughing, for as he straddled her in the back of the van, holding himself against the floor like a man doing press-ups, and she underneath stiff with fright that he might crush her to death, his sword was hanging as humbly as a little Christmas decoration. Finally, she too laughed. Perhaps the van was too constrained a space for their imaginations.

'I'll tell you what,' he announced, sliding over on his back, 'I'll tell you a story instead.'

74

I knew a woman once who had a black-and-white television. And on top of the television she had a stuffed owl and I was sitting on her flea-ridden couch in the front room of her house, staring at the owl.

'Is that a real duck?' I enquired.

'No,' she said, 'that's an owl.'

Then she told me that her husband was forever shooting things and stuffing them.

'It's a sort of hobby with him,' she said, 'the shooting.'

So you see, he shot the owl by accident, for you're not supposed to shoot owls. That's why I pretended it was a duck. But he shot it by accident and brought it home and stuffed it and put it over the fireplace.

Well, some time later he came across a live owl that had blinded itself after crashing into a tree. He took that home as well and the entire family tried to mend its eye and feed it. She had ointment for putting on the children, so that was administered, and behold the owl was healed.

Then they tried to feed it vegetables and meat but it never took anything, until someone told them that an owl has to kill before it eats; so they tied up mice at night and the owl would kill them and make a mighty dinner out of them.

'Well a 'clare ta Gawd,' the woman said, 'it had eyes that would follow you round the house. Even when you were out of sight. But it never moved off its perch for weeks. Until one night there was pandemonium when it flittered the stuffed fella. Bit the ears off and plucked the eyes out.'

'Sure I suppose,' declared Coco, 'it must have been thinking about it for days.'

He had resumed his position above her, nosing against her, and the two swallow's tails of a moustache tickling the face off her. Her body rattled the van then, with delight.

'I'm not happy as a man,' Coco said to her afterwards, uncertain of himself. 'I don't think I have the required prowess.'

But to Sarah he was the finest bull in the world and she patted his enormous head and said, 'You're all right, Coco. You don't have to do anything.'

He was changing the wheel one day and she was admiring him from the passenger-seat window.

'Why do you wear that shirt all the time?' she asked.

'Ventilation,' he shouted from where he was hunched. 'I think, sometimes, that I'm a little girl.'

But from where Sarah was sitting, he didn't look too much like a little girl.

Listen ye daughters of the river,
and remember me.
For I have not forgotten thee,
though the morning be frosty and the ground be hard;
though the window be glazed
and the sharp frosty tongue awakens thee.

There were moments like that when everything made sense to her. From where she watched, his rump shaped itself through the shirt and she had to admit to herself that it was not unlike the elegant hindquarter of a horse. He turned from his work, approached the window and winked into her face.

76

'Don't be shy,' he said. 'Don't be shy.'

Lord Coco was delightfully *au fait* with almost everything. He never had to look at maps and he drove so smoothly that Sarah fell asleep in Meath and didn't wake up till Dublin. He was a dab hand on the ferry. And at Holyhead she was so relaxed that she got into her sleeping bag in the back and completely missed what little there was to see of Wales. The white van made a line through that country, like chalk mark on a blackboard, and when Sarah woke, it was England, and almost London.

'Have you done this before?' she enquired. For she was sorry now she had forgotten her toothbrush.

'All the time,' he replied. He looked across at her and saw the sleep in her face. 'Sure you couldn't make a sparrow's life on Grafton Street,' he said, laughing.

But the big flat English fields and the redbrick stately homes had distracted her.

'Hey, Mustard,' he said, nudging her. 'Dublin – nothing. But Paris, Venice – for Coco – *molti, molti soldi.*' And he pronounced it with an Italian twang and scattered his fingers in the air.

His little bit of mustard, he called her. They were on the boat for Calais; the van was in its chains and clamps in the hole, and unknown to the crew, they lay inside it as it creaked. And they made love there completely and successfully for the first time, and his forcefulness in that darkness made her feel sinful.

Only once did she look back. They went up on deck and leaned over the balcony, and his eyes twinkled and he lit himself a cigar and said in the tones of a small boy, 'I did it that time, didn't I?'

There were lights on the coast of France winking at her. She had surrendered herself to him. In that he had surely done it. It had been impossible at the moment of most intensity not to run her fingers over his shoulders and remember her husband. Very soon now she would be in a foreign land. But what was she doing? In her head she kept saying, Calais means Wordsworth. Calais means there's no turning back. Then her glasses blurred from sea spray and the tears that were forming in her eyes. She felt his fat lips at her ear.

'Don't be afraid,' he whispered, and the words tasted of cigar. 'If you get beyond Calais, you'll be mine for ever.'

He was such a charmer. He looked so ridiculous – a big black coat now over his long shirt, and the shirt and the coat flapped in the wind like blankets. And because he so often sensed what she was thinking, anticipated her and in some unrecognisable way completed her stream of thoughts, she released herself from worry, turned towards him, smiled and allowed his lips to touch hers. Delicate, but it was also like being stung by a big bumblebee; his tongue catching her unawares.

'Come,' he said, 'to the bar.'

The bumblebee in the blankets went down the stairs, his mustard Venus in tow, while many travellers in yellow anoraks, raincoats or Barbour jackets took their eyes off the dark sea for a moment to behold the pair of them with a mixture of astonishment and distaste. Lord Coco and his mustard were for whiskey at the bar and they bounded all the way. And there he revealed his next story.

There was a woman called Jennie. She was a huge big tall woman with grey hair and a Protestant nose. A very big woman. Even as a child she was big-boned and nervous, and liable to bump into the standard lamp.

You see, even at fifty years of age she was still haunted by her father. Years and years after he died. She could still hear him, with his wee baldy head and his sparrow's body, footering around in the room upstairs.

When she'd be staring into the fire in the drawing room or listening to a play on the radio, it could happen suddenly. The furniture in the room would begin to glow. The old botany books on the shelves, which her father so revered, would all. . . glow. And of course the next minute she would hear the unmistakable sound of the floorboards above as the old man travelled across to the pisspot. And this was years after he had died.

Then at a certain stage the trouble began to follow her around the countryside. She used to go to Bundoran for the holidays. Every August. A nice little hotel, and she'd always get a room at the top of the house. But one year, on the first evening, she was sitting in the foyer with tea and a buttered scone when she heard the floorboards creaking above her. Holy Jesus, she thought, it's him.

I know what you're going to say: it could have been anyone in the corridor upstairs. Right? Wrong. That night she went to bed in a room at the top of the house; brushed the teeth, popped into bed, and what do you think she hears but the friggin' whispering in the ceiling. Mice?

Mice, my eye. You see, her father was a good wee man and died as quiet as a bird. Just one afternoon when he was taking a rest upstairs. When it came to seven o'clock and he hadn't come down for his tea, Jennie went up and knocked the door. But there was divil a knock he would ever hear again. She went in and found him as stiff as a poker and his eyes still open.

You see, there was always just herself and the father. And now there was just the father.

But she went to a fortune-teller about it one time. A woman called Mrs Kennedy who had a caravan parked at the corner of the football field one summer during the parish festival. Poor Jennie was very fond of the festivals. It brightened everything up. . .

'Are you all right there? Can I get you another drink? Right.'

. . . Well anyway – the festivals – brightened things up, she used to say. The boys' tin-whistle band marching down the street of the village towards the pitch, followed by the little girls dressed as witches and the boys as girls, and the mammies and daddies straggling along behind with their umbrellas and white hand-bags and raincoats. . .

'What are you laughing at? Oh yes, well of course, sure you would remember the festivals.'

. . . Well anyway – the fortune-teller was one of the entertain-ments and usually her visitors were young girls who wanted to hear a bit of nonsense about the men. . .

'Sorry? Oh you did? Well sure you'd know all about them so.'

. . . But anyway – 'I think I'm haunted,' says Jennie, standing as tall as a giraffe in the fortune-teller's caravan.

Well, the dark-haired Mrs Kennedy just looked at her and scratched her nose and said nothing.

So Jennie repeated herself.

Then there was another pause and Mrs Kennedy said sorry, she only read the cards.

Then there was another occasion when she was talking to an old man in the county home. He was sitting up in bed with a Saint Patrick's Day badge pinned to the lapel of his pyjamas. She mentioned her trouble to him and he just clenched his pipe with his teeth and laughed through his chest and told Jennie to get out of his sight.

Poor Jennie. She got so scared that in the end she wouldn't go up the stairs at all. Used to sleep on the sofa. Went clean off her head listening to those creaking floorboards and of course, in the latter end, she was taken away. To hospital.

The wings of Lord Coco's moustache were sailing through the air as he laughed and his shoulders rocked so much that she was afraid he might crash.

'See?' he said. 'We're in France.'

Sure enough, they were whizzing along on the right-hand side of the road.

'Just mind the road,' Sarah said. She was about to tell him his story wasn't all that funny, but just in time his eye caught hers in a big comical side glance, and she laughed herself. After all, what should she care? She was wheeling through France with a bull-fighter. A man who had balls and was funny.

Of course there were occasions that frightened her. Moments that she did not mention to him, when memory played nasty tricks on her. Like the night in Paris after he had done his tricks outside the Pompidou Centre and she had sat on the cobbles beside his hat, watching the circle throw francs at them. She would hop about on her hunkers gathering them into the hat. But once, she looked up, and there was a face, a face to the back of the crowd that for a second she was certain belonged to her husband. And another time, in a restaurant on the autoroute towards Mâcon, she looked out the window for a second and thought she saw what might have been the back of Doctor Murray's Volvo pulling out and driving away into the night.

On that occasion Coco caught her chin in his hand and pulled it up to his nose. 'There is no one following us, Princess Mustard,' he said.

And to blow away the cobweb of memory, they treated themselves that night to a fancy hotel which had a room cooled by fans on the ceiling, like blades of a helicopter purring above the bed, and a bathroom all to themselves. He was like a walrus in the bath. She stood holding the towel, and then shook talcum powder on him like flour on the dough and slapped it into clouds.

'You look like an angel,' she said.

He stood underneath the fan, smiling at her.

'Do you really want to be a little girl?' she teased.

'Where did you get them?' he asked, his eyebrows lifting as she approached him, her two hands advancing on him with a pair of white lace knickers.

But it wasn't all fun. Her sleep was troubled. She woke him in the middle of the night. 'You never finished,' she said.

'Finished what?' he asked.

'About Jennie.'

He shook the sleep off himself and spoke in a night-time, fruity pillow voice.

Jennie got so frightened of the man upstairs that in the end she wouldn't go up there at all. Not even to the toilet. Convinced as she was that if ever she turned the corner on the landing, his little bald head and red-rimmed eyes would be there staring at her. So she slept under her coats on the couch and used the loo in the back yard, though it was windy on her bottom in winter. And she moved around the house as quiet as a mouse.

Now one day she was in seeing the doctor and there was a man in the waiting room who started to chat with her. He was talking about the night his wife was taken ill.

'I was woken by a noise outside,' he said, 'so I looked out the window and didn't I see herself and Saint Theresa discoursing at the gable of the byre. I knew then that she was dead.'

Well Jennie fairly hopped home that evening with her usual tablets. In the door. And drew all the curtains on the ground-floor windows and vowed never to open them again.

Trouble was that they began to open in her sleep. Each night as she lay on the sofa she dreamt that she woke up and found something making a terrible clatter behind the curtains. She'd go over and open them up and there, between the curtains and the window, would be two brown birds with drab feathers, trying to get out. Then she'd look through the glass and on the other side of the window she could see her father. The rain spilling down on his bald head and his face white with rage as he pointed frantically at the two birds.

Coco brought her to the top of the world. Because it was the way she had gone one time, years ago, as a student – by land over the Alps and down into Turin and on to Venice. He was bringing her the same old route, offering her those times again, with plates of prosciutto and salami, rolls of French bread and litres of wine from bottles without labels.

'Mont Cenis,' he shouted, pointing his finger at the Alps ahead, for she didn't want to go through the dark tunnel of Mont Blanc.

It was like driving up the side of a wall, she thought, and at one stage it was so steep that all their blankets and shoulder bags slid down the floor of the van behind them and hit the back door.

They passed through a wide street with timber houses and beyond it, at the very top, a lake and a pyramid. The van stopped and they both stared out to the right and wondered what a pyramid was doing at the top of the Alps.

'Was it there the last time?' he asked her.

She couldn't remember.

'I always go through the tunnel, meself.'

Then an old grey-haired man in a blue anorak approached the van. Coco asked him was it a pyramid. Of course not. As they unravelled the French phrases, it turned out that the old man was a priest. A Jesuit who was studying flowers and vegetation particular to the Alpine region, and the 'pyramid' was a modern church.

'Aaah, oui,' said Coco, 'je comprennnds.'

Many years ago Napoleon had travelled this way and rested in the old monastery on the other side of the lake. The monastery is only a ruin now, they were told, but the church is still there, which the Jesuit tends, as well as his flowers.

So was there an eating house anywhere nearby?

Yes. *Oui*. Just on down the road a little further.

The priest smiled in the window at Sarah and said hello. Then he turned and went off down the little footpath to his pyramid. Being well above the cloud line, a sudden fog had swept around them in seconds so that the pyramid was only visible in outline and the old ruin, if there was one at all, on the other side of the lake was totally hidden from view. They looked again and the priest had been enveloped by the fog.

Coco flicked on the headlamps and drove off. They spent the rest of that evening and most of the night in a small cosy tavern with crafty wooden furniture and a massive open fire, logs forever being piled on by the man of the house, a fat ruddy-skinned gentleman of about sixty who said little if anything, but nodded respectfully at all the clients whenever he came within a social distance of them. A silent nod, though with the grave authority of an abbot acknowledging the existence of a monk in his presence.

The main cooking was done by the woman. She was no more than a voice which boomed out through the open door of the kitchen. The man came and went through this door, transporting bowls of pasta and bottles of wine to the tables, or dirty dishes to the sink. But the woman resisted making a personal appearance and her invisibility and thundering voice through the door endowed her with an air of quite special authority.

Truly it was a roaring fire, though every log was necessary, as Sarah discovered when she went out to the remarkable hole-in-the-floor loo.

'Jeepers,' she said to him, returning, 'me bum is frozen.'

The meal was extravagant and worked on the basis that you paid the required amount of francs and then ate as much of everything as you liked. There was a long table decked with fish, fruit, vegetables and many sorts of hams and salami, all spread in fans. The centrepiece was a roasted pig, complete with the terror of its final squeal still in its eyes. People prodded, forked, carved and carried all they wanted to their own tables.

Apart from the voice in the kitchen, about which one could not be entirely certain, Sarah was the only woman in the house. The clientele were of two types; on the one hand, truck drivers – French, German, English and Irish – and on the other hand, a group of funny little men with short trousers, pointy hats with feathers, and ruddy cheeks, who were all part of a local shooting club on their annual night out.

As the menfolk became more intoxicated they became wilder. They made eyes at Sarah while rubbing the knife on the sharpener to carve the meat. Ooohing and yahooing and bursting into laughter. Sarah felt their eyes burning up the back of her body but she was none the less inclined to arch her back, exposing as much of her slender neck to them as she could manage.

More booze. And the men in the short trousers getting wilder and wilder. Sending wine to her table and singing choruses of many bawdy songs from the region.

Coco's brown eyes flashed across the table at her. Not jealousy. No. He simply wanted to know if she was getting uncomfortable. In fact Sarah too was becoming expansive with the wine and Sambuca, and the flavour of the pack behind her was sending electric currents through her whole body.

She licked and sucked the dessertspoon longer than was necessary, leaned almost at right angles across the long table when collecting her coffee and moved through the room on her way to pee in such a manner as left the entire room silent, except for a few divine names ejaculated in breathless whispers and in a wide variety of European tongues.

By the time the evening wound up, everybody was pissed out of their skulls. Even the abbot was shedding emotional tears and Coco was simply delighted that she was enjoying herself. An enjoyment that was having an effect on her expression akin to what the blazing sun might do to a drift of snow. The Alpine flowers were blooming.

'You're unwinding,' Coco shouted at her through the singing. She was arm in arm with one of the sharpshooters, poking out the beat of the song on his fat little tummy.

Finally they were alone again and he was about an inch away from her face, gazing into her eyes. She knew he was about to speak.

She lived up the avenue and as a wee girl she was happy; despite her unfortunate disability. You see, as a very young baby she had been burned in the fire, leaving her with a scar on the left side of her face and a dead white eye.

But as I say, she was happy. She'd skip along the avenue in the mornings, going to school, and say to herself that the frost made the pebbles sticky, like marmalade, and the frost made the rhododendron look like sugar sticks.

One day she was walking down the avenue on her way to school, along the road that passes through the wood, when suddenly a young man was standing between two trees beside the road. He was naked.

'You're a nervous little animal,' says he, smiling.

'And who are you?' she asks, for she couldn't understand how he came to be standing there all of a sudden at the edge of the wood.

'I'm the Prince of the Woods,' says he, 'won't you come in and see?'

Well now, she was taking a little peek at his naked thing, so she said, 'I'm afraid I've got to go to school.'

'Oh,' he said, 'please yourself.' And off he went into the dark with a swish.

So all day in school she kept thinking about him. The master nattered on as usual, pacing up and down between the desks and leaning his elbow on the window ledge when he was tired. But going home that evening there were long shadows across the road. She stopped at the spot where she had seen him and she went into the wood. Oh, just a wee bit. To see if she could find him.

'Well fancy that,' says her mother. 'I wonder what your father will say when he hears about naked princes. Naked princes indeed.'

'I'll show ye naked princes all right.' That's all he said as he slashed the legs off her with his stick in the scullery.

Needless to say, though she was yet quite young, that was the night she swore to leave home. Some day, she said to herself, some day.

She began listening to every word that came out of the teacher's mouth. And in the autumn she beat everyone in her class and won a scholarship to the secondary college, where she was sent as a boarder, though her father sniggered at her and said that a nuns' education would be damn all good to her.

In the convent she spent the evenings in the corridors. Looking out windows; hiding from the older girls who called her Dopey, and Cyclops. She would let a long wave of hair fall down her left cheek to hide the scar and the dead eye. But sometimes a nun would insist that she tie it back into a bun, like any respectable girl, and white porcelain hands would pull it all back, in front of the class, revealing the dead eye to the giggles and laughter of the other girls.

She prayed sometimes too, but the only thing she prayed for was not to be hurt.

The letter with her final examination results eventually arrived home one summer's day. And it lay on the oilcloth of the kitchen table all afternoon. Then her father opened it, tossed it at her and watched for the slightest sign of joy. But she stared back at him, for she knew she had beaten him.

'Well,' he said, 'I suppose you're happy now. You'll be getting away from us for good.'

As far as she was concerned, he never spoke a truer word.

So off she went, free as a bird, to the city. Now, she had a long black coat and long fashionable dresses and pretty underwear. And would you believe, her one eye didn't seem to offend anybody. When she began wearing the black patch, it even attracted admiration. The boys thought there was something awfully romantic and heroic about it. And eventually one boy

89

in particular came under her spell. His name was Tommy and he was round-faced, with red hair and freckles. Shy. She had to lead him all the way. When they made love, he was like a man walking in a olive grove, afraid of the ghosts.

Unfortunately he didn't turn out to be much of a hero himself. During the Christmas holidays he wrote to her, saying how much he regretted the liberties he had taken with her. It was wrong. Their intimacy was unwholesome. He begged her forgiveness and hoped they could both put the affair behind them.

It is strange how a little coincidence can sometimes change the entire direction of someone's life. The letter itself would not have crushed her. But she had been feeling unhappy that morning and her good eye had been giving her trouble for over a week. It ran water for a few days and then an unnecessary amount of white puss dribbled from it and trickled down her face. Her vision was blurring and she began rubbing it, and it was getting worse.

No more than anxiety, perhaps, but that letter arrived at an unfortunate moment. The little bastard, she whispered to herself after burning it in the fireplace of her bedroom.

But an hour later she went into town and lit candles in the chapel. She knelt before the outstretched limbs of the suffering Christ and all around she could feel the presence of the father's shadow, beneath which she now bowed and prayed and begged forgiveness.

When she went back to college, she didn't see the little red-haired Tommy any more, nor did her eye trouble her. In fact it was almost a year later before it grew weaker and the specialist said to her that if she didn't take care of it, she wouldn't see next Christmas.

Something inside her had fallen to the ground like a dead tree. She did not go out into the world after college. Far from it. She went home and sat in the kitchen and they all sat around her in the evenings watching her. She was always preparing for the day when she wouldn't be able to see the kitchen wall. She was memorising every detail of the house, in expectation. And during those years she forgot practically everything she had learned and everyone she had known. She even made the effort to erase it. The faces of people she had studied with. The names of places in the university. For it would be too painful to be haunted by those things in the darkness for the rest of her life. And she was preparing for darkness.

She didn't go blind. She just became more and more depressed, until her father said enough was enough – and they put her away in the mental hospital.

When Lord Coco had finished this story, he waited, but she did not laugh. Eventually she said, 'That's not funny,' and he burst out laughing.

They were in a bedroom with massive wooden rafters and a window that looked down upon the Alpine slopes, and an elegant night vase in the locker beside the bed, for there were no toilets upstairs in the hostel.

Coco stopped laughing. He was staring at her like an owl. He had her undressed in a jiffy. His thick purple lips whispered into her face, 'Turn over. . . and lie on your stomach.'

She did this. And again she felt his lips, this time as light as a butterfly, on the back of her ear. After that, his ferocity could not be adequately described.

There are many factors that can impair judgement, cause paranoia and spoil even an ordinary holiday. The rarefied atmosphere of the Alps could have an effect. The strong spices on the exotic foods and the country wine taken to excess. The intimate vocabulary of sexuality can unhinge itself and be carried away in the expression of dark brutality as easily as it can be the exquisite conveyance of tender emotions.

It must be said that when Sarah and Lord Coco descended the rickety wooden stairs the following morning for breakfast, they were both, to put it mildly, a bit shook. Her lips felt swollen and her tongue, as dry as sandpaper. Nor did the morning bowl of coffee help. Coco had the engine of the van running for a full twenty minutes before she finally emerged from the toilet. She sat in stony silence as he drove down into the heat of Italy, still terribly uncomfortable and very specific parts of her anatomy still raw and sore from Coco's teeth and a variety of the night's less orthodox adventures.

Nor did things improve with the day. It seemed as if they were going down for ever. He was driving far too fast. It became hotter and hotter. And as is often the case in such affairs, she remembered more details of the night as the day wore on.

She remembered that they had both woken in the middle of the night and had a discussion about dreams. He dreamt he was a fish swimming up her back, and that her spine was the river bed. She dreamt she was watching a huge bird stretching its wings, blackening her face with its shadow. Then the bird came closer and changed into a fish with wings.

Lord Coco laughed and said that he too had dreamt of a fish that could fly. It came in the window, he said, and gobbled her up. He laughed again. It was the first occasion she resented his laugh. But she slept again. Perhaps for half an hour, perhaps for minutes. When she opened her eyes, he was sitting up in bed watching her.

'I dreamt of another fish,' he said. 'I was catching a pike. I had the cold slippery thing in my hands and I was trying to take the hook from its mouth, but I couldn't.'

She had dreamt that she was inside an enormous goldfish bowl and that he had come towards it, distorted by the glass, his own head on the body of a cat and his giant paw touching the glass. For some reason she didn't tell him this dream.

Now, as they drove along in the van, these dreams returned and frightened her. He was still driving very fast. As if, all of a sudden, he was anxious to complete the journey.

And there was the old question of whether or not they might be followed. Every so often they passed a little blue Fiat full of sleek *carabinieri,* and her stomach knotted and she wondered might those oily young men have her name in their notebooks and a full description of the flamboyant lord's van.

'You're a free woman,' Coco said, 'you can't be arrested for leaving him.'

She closed her eyes and concentrated on the sound of the engine. Trust him, trust him, she kept saying to herself. He knows everything. He's a magician. And then she was tranquil again, as if her innermost thoughts had become like little goldfish.

Now it is possible, in a good vehicle, to traverse northern Italy in a single day if you begin at sunrise and are prepared to drive without stops into the middle of the following night. Coco's van was in excellent condition. He resisted Sarah's pleading to stop for food. Not even a quick sandwich. No. On the last leg of the journey he had become consumed with its completion.

Their destination was a small village in the mountains north of Venice. Some time after Milan they began to veer left. There was something rather sweet about him agreeing to take her back to that village where she had once spent such a happy summer many years ago.

'Sure we will go there,' he said. 'I even have a place there.'

Well of course he didn't have a place there. He couldn't. But Sarah had understood what he meant. He was a travelling man; and he went from place to place; and in that sense he had a place everywhere. Her happy-go-lucky prince.

They say you should never go back anywhere, but it didn't bother Sarah. Her first summer in Europe was the happiest time in her life. Now Coco had brought the long-awaited wind into her life that lifted her sails, and everything would be perfect. Her happy-go-lucky prince. Coco. She refused even to enquire about his real name. No more than she would want him to change his theatrical costume. It was Coco who had taken her away. Coco, with his long ankle-length shirt and his black hat and his magic moustache.

But as already mentioned, this was not a good day for Sarah. No. Not a good day at all, carrying such a hangover across the top of Italy on an empty stomach. The sunshine and heat in the van were oppressive. She was drenched in perspiration and her underclothes stuck to her. Now it was cold and dark again, and the van climbed into the hills and she woke from her half-sleep in a terrible state of fear.

The doubts. The terrible doubts. Had she, in three short days, spoiled her whole life? Had she, in her desperation to have some sort of life, jumped blindfolded off a cliff, only to find herself tumbling hard and fast down onto the rocks? In short – what the fuck had she done?

Oh yes. There was all that. But there was worse. Memory had played one of memory's nasty tricks by waiting until this very moment to bring to her attention an event from the past that ought to have been central to her the previous week – when she was toying on the telephone with a strange man who wanted, as he had said, 'to run away with her'.

Coco was taking Sarah along that route she had travelled one summer as a university student. They had agreed all this and planned it before they left Ireland. It was a village in the mountains. The Dolomites. That's what she had remembered. And apartments were easy to rent. She had once spent the summer of her life there. That's the place. That's where they must go.

'I even have a place there,' he had said. When did he say it? She couldn't remember. At some point in the planning he had said that. Coincidence? But how could he have a place there? No. A man was falling in love with her. A man was opening her out like a flower. Isn't that good enough? Isn't that sufficient reason to close your eyes and leap? But now she remembered.

Among the dusty sloping streets and whitewashed walls and red-tiled roofs and flaking churches there was one dark spot. It was nothing special. Just a big old wooden house on a hill above the village. The locals said it belonged to the 'Englishman', and when Sarah and her young companion had suggested with enthusiasm that they might pay a visit, the locals were horrified.

'No, no,' they had protested, 'the Englishman likes no visitors.'

From that day onwards the wooden house overlooking the village was like a shadow. They never saw anyone come or go from it, never saw a curtain move or a light go on at night, but every time they thought of it, they got the shivers, and whenever they went walking in the mountains, they walked every way except the road that passed the house of the Englishman.

Now there is a time in every story when the listener runs ahead of the speaker, and this moment may be upon us. For who is to say what lay ahead for Sarah? It is possible that when the van finally came to a halt beside that dilapidated mansion and Coco had opened the old door with his comical key, Sarah found everything to her taste. A bottle of wine and a roll of bread with a few slices of *mortadella* purchased at the *alimentari* as they passed through the village might all have loosened Coco's tongue.

Perched between the flame light of two candles, he might have spoken of his devotion to her – even in the far past; of his wealth and education, for which this street persona was merely a whimsical smoke screen. She might have glanced about the kitchen and found it clean and homely; the huge medieval mantelpiece decked with books on Venetian choral music. And he might have looked his best there in such a light – bullish and romantic, and not at all out of place to be sporting such clothes or such a moustache.

It might have been the night on which he swore to her his undying love and devotion, and arranged to meet solicitors the following day in order to dignify her position in his company.

And coitus that night? With the buzz of the wine?? Surely the Song of Solomon itself could not adequately describe the grip and tumble of their waking and dreaming till the sun rose over the hills and lanced the milky fog on the planes around Venice.

She would rise from their bed and draw just a sheet about her shoulders and tiptoe barefoot through the curtains, to lean over the balcony of their bedroom. In a moment he is beside her, proud as a lion, naked and full of swagger.

Down there, he would say to her, pointing at the vast land-scape, is the world.

She might wriggle her toes on the timber beneath her feet and smile at it all and say to him I'm home at last.

And he would say, yes indeed you are.

And what a breakfast he might make for her then! But who is to say?

On the other hand, there is no need to spell out the litany of possibilities available to the darker side of Coco. Suffice it to say that Man has come far since the Renaissance. Or perhaps it was ever so. Stretch your imagination far enough to incor-porate every technicality of psychological and physical torture that makes common reading in the daily papers, marry these to the unhappy fact that there is in the human condition an appetite to congress most brutally and to experience the Love Object as victim, and you will have no doubt in your mind that Sarah had placed herself in an extremely vulnerable position.

No one in the world, except this clown, knew where she was. What lay ahead? Within the many rooms of his lonely mansion, what instruments, manacles, belts or buckles? No one could possibly tell. Except himself. What fancies smouldered behind his eyes? Behind the eyes of a man who had the strength of a horse, who roamed the highways and byways of Europe in a van festooned with the paraphernalia of an aging hippy, and who dressed himself like a clown in a long nightshirt? What indeed smouldered there? No one, perhaps not even himself, could tell. Sarah had already been exposed to the sharper edge of his sword and she had noticed just the faintest whiff of a kinky smoke. Now as the van stopped outside a shop she was saying to herself that where there is smoke, there may or may not be fire.

What village they stopped in is hard to say. Their presence went unnoticed. The van stopped for no more than five minutes. He bought a loaf of bread and a litre of wine. Red. He was lucky. It was nearly ten o'clock and the man was about to pull down the steel shutter on his shop front.

The van continued. Up the ribbon road, around the hills, in the direction of Coco's house. The sticker on the rear window exhorting all to make love and not war. But what awaited her as the van became a dot and vanished and finally the hum of its engine faded from the quiet street — no one, no one at all, can tell.

CASNAGEE

Oh now,
says the vet, sitting at the bar in the hotel,
oh now, it was a pity about her.
Aye.
And y'know, he was such a nice young fella.
James. Aye.
James was such a nice young fella.

And a' course, Mrs Gullion. Kitty. The Mother.
Aye.
There's the woman that put in the hard life.

D'ye know what I'm goin' to tell ye?
That woman is a saint.
Now.

I think she came originally from Omagh.
And then sure she hadn't them half reared when
ould Gullion was got dead in the bed. Aye.
But be cripes, she reared them, the lot of them,
and put every single wan of them through college.

And a quare good religious woman too.
Mrs Gullion.
Oh shockin'.
Very attentive. To the prayers.
Well Jesus, Mary and Joseph, she'd pray. Ah now.

Then a' course the sons were just that bit

headstrong
about the politics.
If ye get me.

Aye.

Ah well, sure you'll have that.
But they say there was no better woman
nor wee Kitty.
And then, when the husband died and she got the car,
sure she'd pick up anyone and everyone on the road.
Pucks a' them.
Going to Mass.

Ah sure look, that woman, if ye were in difficulties,
and I can talk,
that woman was a walking charity. . .

There were times in that bar when there were so many shorts of
whiskey on the counter that if a member of the Pioneer Total
Abstinence Association were to as much as breathe, he'd be
breaking his pledge.

Ah well, that's all right,
says the draper to the vet,
but on the contrary,
she fenced in all that mountain land
to keep the neighbours out.
And she niver did nothing in relation to the son
without consulting a solicitor.

D'ye unnerstand?

An' I'll tell ye more,
for I know.
She had a bank account on the other side of the border,

so that she wouldn't be getting too entangled
with the tax people.

If ye get me drift.

And in fact, if the truth were told,
then it's fair to say
that if things weren't good
for the same Kitty Gullion,
then the same wee Kitty
wouldn't be so good.

And of course
there's people say that some things isn't lucky.

Meaning nothing in particular.

But there was that time
when she crossed the priest
about James's wedding;
when there was an altercation
about the photographer
at the ceremony.

Oh the sun shone out of Sarah's backside
in them days all right.

Well I'm tellin' ye, some things isn't lucky.
That's all.
And looka' how it's turned around. . .

There were times too in that hotel when the company at the bar
would fall silent and drink deeply.

D'ye remember the time,
says the milkman,

when the man came from the Department
while she was in the middle of the dinner?

Be jaypers, she lost half the herd that time.
Half the fuckin' herd. . .

That was true.

And the winter afterwards,
says the cobbler,
didn't James crash the Datsun,
and him not insured?

Oh, but but but,
says the vet, rallying now,
I mind all that well, but be Jeezis, I niver heard a
word out of her only that God was good. . .

And by jingo, that swung the opinion round, for they all raised
their glasses and agreed that Kitty Gullion was the first class of
a lady.

A finer woman nor wee Kitty ye couldn't meet, they said.
Oh now, they agreed, the poor woman got a lot of hard knocks.
But none harder than this.
This what?
Ah Jeezis, amn't I tellin' ye?
The trouble with the Sarah wan. James's woman.
Whatever the fuck he got entangled with her for in the first
place?
That's the mystery.

Oh it's a true saying – marry on the dung hill.

Don't get it wrong.
There's good and bad in everyone.
Sarah, or Kitty Gullion. . .

Sarah let herself be led, through gardens and glasshouses, and flung headfirst against the wall. She couldn't see that they would blame her.

Inside herself she was divided. Something ran right down the middle, cutting her in two. There was a side to her that was lush and green and hungered for growth. Some little shape within. And at the other end of her was a space marked out by the doctor. He pointed to it each time he examined her. With fierce curiosity.

And she allowed him to.

He would give it a classical name; and she couldn't understand his fingers, but they soiled her and she would not cry out.

She thought she needed him, and his scholarship,
and his cherry tree.
She thought she could keep herself in two halves.
And in the half the doctor didn't touch she had something like a garden where she could run through, in dreams; spaces where she could touch the most elegant shapes in creation.
Sometimes in the library or in the hospital she thought she might turn into a flower.
A flower could read anything, she thought.
A flower could say yes to any atrocity
and not care.
And at night, from the kitchen window of the bungalow,
she could see the moon over the lake
in the valley below.
A still pond like a wound in the earth,
being healed all night by the dense woods
that skirted the shoreline.

Such innocence.

Like the time she began sitting in the greenhouse all day long with the plants, knitting. That would give her strength, she thought. But sitting on the doctor's porch was bad enough; knitting in the greenhouse, with the tomatoes, gave him all the cause he wanted.

I'm telling yis,
from the very first day she set foot in that bungalow
she was a droll creature. . .

And of course the bungalow is still there. Even if we were to slip five years on down the road, the paint on its walls would be relatively fresh.

But Sarah is not there. And perhaps she is not in Italy either. Who is to say? Perhaps no such white van ever came for her, but an ambulance, to bring her to hospital, where she lies year in year out on a silver bed, her mouth puffed out, her eyes yellow and glazed and staring at the ceiling.

Taking her tablets. A good patient in ways. Obedient. The half of her that Doctor Murray first fingered and diagnosed now enlarged so that it is the entirety; and the other half as dry as dust in an empty well. A hollow, echoing only sometimes with the distant ranting of another lunatic in the corridor: Terry Hill from Donegal, known affectionately as Errigal the Oracle on account of his inclination to stand in his pyjamas in the corridor any time he gets the chance and accost the infrequent visitors with his ludicrous truth:

> Listen to me all ye daughters of Ulster,
>   for the axe is already to the root of the tree.

But who is to say?

Definitely not the boys in the hotel. If they thought Mrs Gullion would have keeled over and died because of the trouble with the daughter-in-law, then they were far from the truth.

Mrs Gullion's in her eighties. Came over to live with James. Doesn't go out much nowadays, but by all accounts she cooks, cleans and is, as they say, thriving on it.

James seems happy enough too. The war goes on. The farm

does well. He has another new car and he bought the mother a colour television, and often the two of them sit there at nights, in the drawing room, watching the news. Together. They're very keen on the news, the pair of them. Especially if there's anything of, shall we say, a local interest, like the time Joey blew up the barracks. Oh yes. Joey is no eejit nowadays. A term inside and then released. It's a long war. Joey is no eejit. Or the time that Remembrance Day affair got hit at Enniskillen. Now there was a night they were watching the box with keen interest. It was, after all, very much their story.

EPILOGUE

'The moment will never end.
She will never take her eyes off me.
There will be nothing left in her
when I have finished.

'I will have her.
I will.
And she'll sing no poetry then,
me little bride,
my silver medal,
my come-down-the-morning-early-woman.

'I'll shove my fist in and gouge it out.
Scrape it clean till she is like an empty prayer bowl.
Till there is nothing left she can see.
Till she knows no better than to cry out
have pity please, have pity.

'I'll give her the goats
and the deer stags.
Her, with her galivanting.
I will.
And I'll banish the little flock
of children's voices
fluttering in her.
I will.

'I'll have her.
Wait till you see.'

Oh yes, but she was never quit praying for one thing or another.
If it wasn't just the nerves, it was the trouble with the bladder.
And if it wasn't just the bladder, it was the trouble in the yard.
One thing on top of the next, slithering up the long *res lubrica*.

She is always there. Lying in a room, her eyes towards heaven
or the ceiling. When she sleeps, she sleeps in a river. When she
wakes, she keeps her mouth shut.
A feather on the pool.
A coffin on the river.
Nothing to fear but the fellow who comes into the yard.
That's the night she goes down on her knees, and hopes every-
thing will turn out right.

And she learns to pray with her face to the wall.

'Oh but I'll take no chances with ye,
no,
I won't.
You'll hold nothing back.
Not a devotion will you hold
any time
of the day or night.
You fuckin' won't.

'And boys, will you run?
Run,
look, run
and knock all the bloody doors
you like,
but you'll deliver yourself up to me
in the end.
In the latter end.'

Everywhere she is cloistered
by the walls of a bungalow or a semidetached.
Feeling each day prettier than ever.

Waiting.
Always waiting for him to turn the key in the door.
And every night she watches the news,
like a dry weary land without water.

She waits for the leaves to fall
and the bone to wind through the place where the leaves were.
She waits for the corpse
draped in its flag,
holding her cigarette out
to the wind.

Like a black rock she waits
for bones breaking in the night;
for boats in a storm;
like a woman in a lounge bar
waiting for her husband.
Waiting to be pregnant.

She is like wallpaper.
The flowered patterns have eased into her marrow.
Her days whirlwind up tunnels of sycamore.

She is sparrow-cocked down corridors
in night journeys;

hospital clocked,
she wanders about
in her pyjamas
looking for the lavatory.

'But you're not listening, child.
You don't listen.
For I can see you
crumble yet
and ask for protection.
Sooner or later you'll dip your nose

in the honey pot
and you'll be cornered then,
by dad.
Ready to unload your little secrets.'

The game is almost up.
He has announced his entry into her house.
The house of the bad odours.
His claw is on the banister.
He is mounting the stairs.

'I'll give her perfumes,' he says, 'I'll give her juices.
I'll give her all the juice she wants.'

She saw him once at the gable of the street. He came as close
as the back door. And she knew it was him, for he bared his
upper teeth when he laughed, and he laughed a lot
when he saw her squatting on the floor.
And when he was around,
she was frightened at night
by the sounds
in the yard.

He opens the door
of the room where she sleeps.
She untightens her naked body
to accept him.

Accept him?
Accept him?
Can it really be possible that in the end she
accepts him?
As he approaches the bed,
reaches his arm out over her naked body
and blows
blows,
blows

blows,
blows blows blows
her fucking head off.

Seven rounds.

To make sure.

Christ have mercy on me, she says,
Lord have mercy
Christ hear me
Christ graciously hear me.
Angel at the window
pray for me
house of the sleepers
pray for me
sticks of light
pray for me
cracks in the silence
pray for me.

All ye who live in the cloister and the woods
pray for me.
All ye who go out in boats
pray for me.

From the dream that withers
O Lord deliver us
From the face in the pool
O Lord deliver us
From the names and addresses
O Lord deliver us
From the warrior who cuts the tree to the root
O Lord deliver us
From the hole in the ditch
and the man in the river
O Lord deliver us

Christ deliver us
Christ hear us
Christ deliver us
Christ graciously hear us.

She said.

She would have said more but she hadn't time.

Scatter.
That's what they say when a target is hit.
Scatter.
And the man who did it would fuck off,
his hammer still up
and his throat full of pride.
His prayers like a flock of dead birds.

So now the soldier knows everything about her.
Her name,
and her lips.
Her veils and her tents.

And the look in her eyes
as she died.